# Intrigue

*A Regency Romance*

**TITLES BY JAIMEY GRANT**

**Connected Regencies**:

Honor
Betrayal
Deception
Intrigue
Entangled (Spellbound)
Heartless
Redemption
Forgotten, and other Heartless tales

**Short Stories**:

My Lady Coward: An Episodic Regency Romance
The 11th Commandment: A Serial Romance
Death Becomes Her: a Gothic tale
*The Devil She Knows* in Death Becomes Her
*Assassin's Keeper / Survival* in Unlocked: Ten "Key" Tales
*Eliza's Epiphany* in Whispered Beginnings
The Dragon's Birth (fantasy)

# Intrigue

*A Regency Romance*

by

## JAIMEY GRANT

TreasureLine Publishing

*Intrigue*
A Regency Romance
by Jaimey Grant

Cover design by Laura J Miller
www.anauthorsart.com
Stock photos from
www.periodimages.com
www.depositphotos.com

Published by TreasureLine Publishing
www.treasurelinebooks.weebly.com

First published 2013
EAN-13: 978-1-61752-174-4

Printed in the United States of America.

# Intrigue

*A Regency Romance*

# PROLOGUE

*Summer 1819*

The carriage lurched to a halt amid curses and neighing horses.

"Stand and deliver!"

The lone passenger, a striking woman in her early thirties, sucked in a breath and screamed. Her voice reverberated in the small space, threatening to permanently damage her own hearing.

With a prayer trembling on her lips, she stepped down from the conveyance, her movements shaky and unsure. She stood, cowering and miserable, as the thieves rifled through her reticule and rummaged through the carriage.

As the moments passed, she began to relax, thinking maybe, just maybe, her prayers had finally been answered.

The sound of approaching hooves put paid to any such notion. Her stomach sank to her sensible halfboots as a man on a horse charged into the fray, brandishing a pistol and threatening the bandits with any number of dire consequences should they refuse to cease their theft.

A scream rose up in the victim's throat, a cry of anguish and warning, quickly swallowed, hastily suppressed. If the boy simply let them take what they wanted and go, everyone would be safe.

As three other armed men stepped from the trees, the young man on the horse was made quickly aware that he was in over his head. He tossed his pistol aside as ordered and leapt down, more than willing to part with a few meager possessions in exchange for his life.

And that of the lady, too, of course.

When his pockets were emptied, one of the bandits made the young man kneel, adding humiliation into the mix. A gun was placed to his head.

The lady's breath caught in her throat, unease making her stomach clench in pain.

She stepped forward. The bandit with the gun looked at her, his eyes dead in his gaunt face. She hesitated only briefly; she did not want anyone hurt. If she could stop this, she must try.

Just as she opened her mouth to protest, a shot rang out. She watched helplessly as the body of a boy not much older than her own son fell lifeless to the ground.

*Months later...*

Gideon could hardly believe his luck when he came upon the holdup. It was just what he needed to relieve the truly abominable *ennui* he'd been cursed with of late.

His eyes scanned the area. The lady appeared the typical vaporish female with more hair than wit, though he couldn't accurately judge either simply from seeing her bonneted form wreathed in moonlight. Her attackers lounged about, saying little, seeming bored and unenthusiastic about their task. What the devil were they waiting for?

It was an odd situation and just the thing to appeal to a man of Gideon's mercurial temperament.

He pulled Black to a halt. The horse did his best imitation of a statue, the flick of his ear the only indication of life.

Gideon dismounted silently, letting the reins drop to the ground. He crept around the robbery, assessing the situation. One band of robbers held the woman, but another was surrounding them.

Footpads who preyed on footpads? Gideon supposed such a thing, though unlikely, was possible. It didn't answer the question of why the ones holding the woman acted as though they waited for something.

Or perhaps they awaited *someone*.

He had to remove two of the gun-toting thieves before he could get close enough to the woman who was, thankfully, near the bushes along one side of the road. He made a sound that got her attention. She shrugged at the man who held her at gunpoint. Gideon's pale brows lifted.

A strange development, indeed. The little beauty was obviously in league with the villains. The intelligent thing was for him to ride away and search out the widow he needed to locate. If this girl was one of the villains, she'd not be hurt and the Home Office wanted him watching the widow as soon as may be.

But this girl was obviously a lady. A rich cloak fell in graceful folds over her proud form, expensive jewels glinting with her every movement in the pale moonlight. Nothing in her expression—what he could make out in the meager light—indicated a willing accomplice. Perhaps they were using her as a means to an end.

When the gunman turned away, Gideon snaked out an arm and snagged the girl, clapping a hand over her mouth before she released the scream he knew was hovering on her pretty lips. He heard the immediate shout go up and cursed.

"If you do not scream, woman, we may yet get out of this alive."

Screaming was exactly what Lady Malvina Brackney wanted to do. She swiveled her head to look at the man who'd dared accost her. Night-darkened eyes gazed back at her in lazy amusement. She had only a moment to feel outrage before good sense came to her rescue. Nodding, she found her hand firmly clasped and then they were running through the trees. Malvina had to keep all her wits about her to avoid tripping over her own two feet and the many branches and animal holes along the way.

They broke out of the trees. A large, dark horse stood complacently near the road, blending into the shadows. The beast waited while Malvina's rescuer threw her into the saddle and mounted behind her. Wrapping one arm around her, he pulled her tight against him. He said something in a tongue she didn't recognize that set the horse off at a smooth gallop. Once the beast broke into a run Malvina knew her tormentors would never catch them.

She shifted just enough to get a look at the man who held her. All she could see in the moonlight was a pair of eyes gazing back at her. Suppressing a shiver of unease, she returned her eyes to watch where they were going.

A few miles from the scene of the holdup, he slowed the horse to a walk.

"Who are you?" she ventured to ask.

"Who are you?" he countered, his tone containing the barest hint of amusement.

"I asked you first."

"And you'll answer first, too, I think."

Astounded at his effrontery, she swung her upper body around so fast she'd have unseated herself if not for his restraining arm around her middle. Unnerved, she couldn't suppress the anger in her words. "What, sir, makes you think that?"

There was so little she could tell about this man. He was a gentleman, of that she was sure. The night hid everything except the glint of gold on his head. The man wore a hat but he'd pushed it back on his head, allowing shafts of moonlight to caress his hair. Gold curls, from what she could deduce.

He shrugged, the movement brushing his body just a bit closer to hers. "The appearance of a magistrate."

She felt her face drain of color and hoped the pale light of the moon didn't reveal it. "I wish one would appear. I'd like to lodge a complaint about how unsafe it is to travel," she claimed with false bravado. "First I am held up by dangerous highwaymen and then I am accosted by a madman who seems to find the whole situation immensely funny."

As if to solidify her claim, her captor laughed. "You have not been accosted, madam, at least not by me. What your highwaymen did before I arrived I cannot possibly know."

Was it her imagination, or did he place just the faintest emphasis on the word highwaymen? She struggled to keep any emotion from showing on her face, not entirely convinced the darkness would hide what she revealed. She turned away just to be safe.

"You, madam, are full of secrets, I think." Her head whipped around again. He stared at her. "And older than I first thought."

Unaccountably hurt by this observation, Malvina lashed out, "And you are nothing more than a boy playing at hero!"

The lazy amusement disappeared for a moment, replaced by something that made her shiver. His body tensed, his entire being emanating disapproval, even anger. He appeared extremely dangerous in that moment. It was gone almost instantly and she shook her head. Perhaps it had merely been a trick of the moonlight.

"Perhaps," he replied equably, looking away. "But everyone needs to be doing something."

Malvina fell silent, staring straight ahead again. The stillness of the wood surrounded her, sending a shiver down her spine.

"Are you cold?" her rescuer asked solicitously. He pulled her closer to his warm body.

She stiffened. "I am not, sir. Please loosen your grip."

He laughed. "I'd rather not if it's all the same to you. I like having you here."

Mouth dropping open, she swung around, nearly unseating herself in the process. Again. "How dare you! Who do you think you are?"

"I am a man, madam. Surely you did not expect better?"

She turned away. "I suppose I should not. You have kidnapped me, sir, and that alone would proclaim you anything but a gentleman."

"I *kidnapped* you?" he asked softly, ignoring the slur on his honor.

Malvina didn't look at him and so missed the sharp look in his eyes. "Of course, I thank you for rescuing me, but did you have to take me away as well?"

"I saw no other recourse, madam. What would you have had me do? Leave you to face your employer's wrath for having lost a very fat purse?"

Gideon regarded her blandly. There was real fear in her bearing, fear and wariness. When would she finally reveal her identity? He already had his suspicions.

That would be a problem, if his suspicions proved true. He was sent to make the acquaintance of a certain lady, a lady whose late husband's actions had caught the eye of certain government officials.

"I do not know what you are talking about," she said. There was an uncertainty in her tone that was quite convincing but Gideon heard a slight tremble at the end, as if she couldn't manage to feign confusion anymore.

"Where shall I take you?" he asked, in a seeming *non sequitur.*

"Take me?"

"Yes, madam. Have you a home? Perhaps a place you can stay for the nonce? I would offer to allow you stay with me, but I don't think you'd like the suggestion."

"No, I would not."

"Well, then. Whereto?"

"Drop me here. I shall find my way."

"How old are you?" he asked with much amusement.

Outraged, she glared at him. "That is none of your business, sir!"

"I only ask because you appear to be a woman grown, yet you display the intelligence of a small child."

Her mouth dropped open but no words emerged. He smiled blandly at her, waiting politely for her to continue. She turned away instead.

He bowed to instinct.

Leaning forward until his lips nearly pressed to her ear, he whispered, "Everything about you is of concern to me, Lady Malvina Brackney."

2

"How did you know?" Disbelief colored every word.

"I merely speculated," he replied with a sudden yawn. He drew the horse to a halt. "Are you sure you would like to be dropped here? I could take you home, you know."

Stunned by his assumption and his sudden attitude of unutterable boredom, Malvina just stared at him.

How was any of this happening? How had she gone from an ordinary widow with a son to this desperate woman willing to trust a man she'd never met? When had she become such a stranger?

She shook her head. "Since you know where I live, sir, you may as well take me home."

The horse started off with one softly spoken word from his master, ambling along with every appearance of being just as complacent as the man on his back.

Where had he been bound when he happened upon the holdup? He seemed to know the area quite well.

"Have you a relative in the area, sir?" she asked.

"Curiosity will be the death of you, Lady Brackney," he replied unhelpfully.

Malvina fell silent for a moment, unsure how to react to such a response. Then, "Are you threatening me?"

"I would never threaten a lady, ma'am."

His tone seemed to imply that she wasn't a lady though his face revealed nothing in the dim moonlight. She opened her mouth to respond when he suddenly informed her that she was home.

She slid from the horse with his help and stood on the ground looking up at him. "Thank you, sir, for your timely intervention. And thank you for returning me to my home."

Plans must be made if Malvina was to successfully maneuver her way out of the bumblebroth she'd landed in. Someone was going to be very displeased when he discovered tonight was ruined and Malvina did not care for his displeasure at all.

The man dismounted, much to Malvina's surprise, and bowed low before her. "Are you not going to invite me in, my dear lady?"

Her mouth dropped open. "No, sir, I am not! What kind of lady do you think I am?"

He bent closer to her but the encroaching darkness threw his expression into shadow. "I know exactly what kind of *lady* you are, madam. If you have any care for yourself or your son, you will invite me in, as we have much to discuss."

His intense, serious tone jarred her, sending shivers down her spine. It lacked his earlier air of boredom, hinting at a much harder man within.

"You *are* threatening me," she breathed. Whatever would she do if he chose to hurt her? Her gaze darted around, looking for something, anything that might serve as a weapon.

He leaned back, his lazy grin reappearing. "I do not threaten, my lady. I find the business far too fatiguing."

Malvina stared, unsure what to make of her companion. He flashed from amusement to anger in the blink of an eye, teased one moment and threatened the next. His stance spoke of tightly leashed energy, yet there was a certain ease to his lanky frame that made no sense. He was a contradiction, a man she didn't understand and couldn't control.

And he wanted to enter her home.

Her mind screamed at her to flee, run as far and as fast from this man as her legs could carry her. But her heart, traitorous thing that it was, whispered other things, things she'd not dared think of since her husband's death, things she had no business thinking about an exciting stranger she'd just met—or not met as the case may be.

Feeling she had little choice in the matter, she invited him in.

Gideon gazed around the spacious residence of his reluctant hostess. Her home screamed poverty. The furnishings, though of the first stare at one time, were threadbare and old. The tapestries that lined the walls of the entryway were badly in need of a thorough cleaning. The floor upon which they stood was dirty and appeared to have been that way for some time.

His gaze settled on her as she removed her fancy little bonnet. Lustrous red curls rioted all over her head, refusing to remain restrained in the knot at her nape. Rich garnets graced her throat, the color repeating in the velvet trim on her pelisse and gown. What was this woman involved in that allowed her to dress so richly while her home moldered and fell about her ears?

With a sideways glance at the villainous looking butler who had reluctantly allowed him entrance, he murmured, "I would suggest you fire this lazy lot and hire new servants, ma'am."

"I cannot," she snapped. Consternation clouded her features. "They have been servants here for many years and I think it would be cruel to dismiss them."

"If they were old, I might understand that," he said, watching the way her gaze darted about and her fingers clenched at her sides. What reason could she have for lying? "But they are not. They are, from what I have seen, all fit individuals, clearly able to undertake the jobs required of them to make this house run properly." At that moment, two maids entered the hall, chatting furtively, and exited by way of a door just down the way. Gideon stared after them, then looked down at his hostess. "Do you not agree, my lady?" he murmured.

"What do you care, sir? You are as lazy as they are," she retorted.

He grinned. "True, true. But, when you visit my home, you will see that my servants are not."

"What do you mean, *when*?" she asked as she led him to the door through which the two maids had disappeared.

Gideon shrugged. "Who knows?"

She turned so quickly that Gideon didn't have time to react. She ended up in his arms and he couldn't have been more surprised—or pleased. A strange sensation filled him, a feeling of rightness that couldn't possibly be real. He reasserted his usual air of lazy boredom, forcing back the inappropriate sensations. He grinned down at her, watching a range of emotions pass through her pale green eyes.

"Release me at once, sir!" she commanded, pushing at his arms with little result.

"Why?" he asked, truly curious. Her eyes widened, lips pinching in at the corners. As her fingers clenched on his arms, he realized what he was seeing. Fear.

He released her and stepped back. "We must talk," he murmured, looking around. The maids stood in the drawing room, watching them with acute interest. A footman lingered behind them in the corridor listening unashamedly and the butler was still within hearing distance. He leaned forward, whispering in her ear, "Do you trust your servants?"

"No, sir, not at all." She appeared surprised at her own admission.

He muttered a curse. Why had he not thought about that when he realized who she was? Probably because he had believed her guilty just as his superiors did. "They are not really your servants, are they?" he asked, assuming they were her husband's.

"No," she said. "But it is useless for us to talk. I do not even know who you are."

He looked down at her with a sweet smile. "I am someone who wants to help you," he whispered, his eyes sweeping her lush form. An idea blossomed in his mind that he couldn't help but admire. "Do you trust me?"

Her eyebrows shot upward, then back down into a frown. "I barely know you. But you did save me from—"

Before the last words were out of her mouth, Malvina found herself being thoroughly kissed. She protested until she felt the warning pressure of his hand at her waist. So she stood very still and allowed him to do what he wanted until his tongue pushed past her lips. Strange heat spread through her limbs at the intimate contact, a remembered sensation from early in her marriage.

But this time it was different. This man was different, more exciting, intriguing, and appealing than her late husband. Her attraction to him was illogical and inappropriate, but she had no desire to stop, no desire to think.

Instead of pushing him away with indignant exclamations of outrage, she drew him closer, kissing him back. He swept her up into his arms, his lips never leaving hers, and carried her up the stairs. Their surroundings melted away until it was just them, alone, nothing to interfere or shatter the—.

He tore his lips away to ask, "Which room is yours?"

Malvina came back down to earth with a rude bump. What she had just done, what she had allowed him to do, rushed in on her. Without thought for the consequences, she reached up and dealt him a stinging blow. He pushed open the first door and let go of her, his brown eyes hard as rock. The door slammed behind him as she landed on the floor with a thump. A pained cry ripped from her throat and she glared up at him.

"You, my lady, are sorely in need of a lesson in gratitude," he bit out, a red hand print appearing on his cheek.

Then, before her very eyes, he once again became the lazily smiling man she'd come to expect.

"Is this your chamber?" he asked with apparent interest, his gaze sweeping the cozy chamber.

Malvina tried to form a coherent thought. One moment her entire being was taken up with sensations she'd thought long dead, and the next she was picking herself up off the floor, shaking out her skirts and resisting the urge to rub her smarting backside. Anger coursed through her, some directed at him but most of it reserved for herself for responding to his kiss in such an abandoned manner.

Finally, she forced words passed her clenched teeth. "Yes, it is. I don't know what you think you... Wait! You are the one who insulted me, kissing me in such a disgusting way! I demand an apology, sirrah!"

The infuriating man grinned and deposited himself in a chair by her bed. "I apologize for disgusting you, my lady. I was unaware that Beowulf was an Immaculate Conception. I was under the impression that Christ was the only human able to lay claim to that."

"That is not what I meant, and you know it, sir," she returned, blushing hotly despite her best efforts to resist. "And we will not speak of my son."

He shrugged, a careless gesture she was coming to hate. "Do you suppose someone listens at the door?"

His shifts in topic dizzied her. A headache blossomed behind her eyes. "I do not know. No one enters here other than my maid and we speak as little as possible." She sat on the bed and then wished she had chosen anywhere else.

His eyes lingered on bed, sending a nervous quiver through Malvina's belly.

"You have no lover? I am shocked," he told her, looking far more sleepy than shocked.

"What have I done to occasion such insult, young man?" She kept her tone neutral, as if they were discussing the most mundane of topics, though she wanted to scream.

"That remains to be discovered, madam," he answered just as blankly. He threw a quick glance at the door. "We have approximately four minutes before we will be interrupted by your diligent maid." His gaze flew back to her. "I am here to offer help, my lady. Whether or not you accept it is on you. But I warn you, if you refuse, your life as you know it will end."

Her brows shot up. "How melodramatic."

Her companion's expression didn't change. His eyes remained steady on hers, nothing to indicate that he found any amusement in her remark.

"Dramatic or not, it is the truth," he told her. "You and your son are in danger."

Malvina felt the blood drain from her face. "Are you threatening me?"

"If that is what it takes for you to see sense, I am."

She stood, rage shuddering through her. "I want you to leave, you scoundrel! You are not welcome here and if you dare to threaten me again, I will see you taken up by the magistrate!"

"I am very much afraid you cannot do that, my lady," he said with infuriating calm. He gazed at her through half closed, sleepy eyelids, smiling slightly. "You see, it is the law that you need to fear and I am the only one who can save you." His smile widened. "In fact," he added, "I am the only one who cares enough to try."

She sat down again with a bump. He was pleased to see he had effectively captured her attention. "What can you mean?" she whispered.

How much should he tell her? His instinct told him she was innocent but he'd seen far too many men die for following just such an instinct. Usually at the hands of a consummate actress.

He rose from his chair and crossed the room until he stood just before her. She leaned back slightly. Her pleasing features took on a questioning expression, pale brows forming a V above her eyes.

He took her hand and pulled her to her feet. "We are about to be interrupted," he told her calmly. Then he clasped her around the waist and kissed her with far more skill than before and for far longer. He actually felt he would quite like kissing her for the rest of his life. And for claiming to dislike the practice, he thought with amusement, she was very good at it.

The door opened, just as he had predicted, the lady's maid sticking her head through.

Gideon lifted his head and stared down into Lady Brackney's eyes, secretly delighting in the look he saw there. He was man enough to feel some satisfaction that he had managed to affect her so much. A silent message passed between them and he felt her shiver at the look of anger that suddenly suffused his features.

He let go of her and swung around, his body blocking hers from the servant's view. "What the devil do you want?" he demanded of the startled maid.

"I was to check on her ladyship," she replied, a hint of scorn in her tone.

"You've done that, now she wants to be alone," he said with implacable conviction.

The maid looked at Lady Brackney for confirmation. Gideon glanced down at her with an unmistakable demand and warning in his eyes.

Malvina knew what he was trying to say. This was when she was to make her decision to accept his help or send him packing. She realized she would do anything to get away from *That Man* and she knew that her continued association with *That Man* was detrimental to her son's health and happiness, maybe even his life.

But she also knew that by telling the maid to leave, she was announcing to the world that she had taken a lover. As much as the loss of her reputation sickened her, she considered it a small price to pay for the safety of her only child.

"Leave, Hilda," she commanded firmly. She saw something flare momentarily in the brown eyes of her companion and looked away. "I will call you when I have need of you," she added, sealing her fate.

As the maid left, Malvina wondered if the nameless male before her would actually take advantage of the situation and make their affair a reality. Horror washed over her when she realized she hoped he would try. His eyes revealed nothing, however, and she waited for him to speak.

"Well done, Lady Brackney," he said with a sleepy smile. He returned to his seat and stretched his long legs out before him. "And now, I think you should tell me exactly what it is you are involved in."

"Can you not tell me who you are?" she asked. Instead of sitting again on the bed, she went to sit across from him in the chair that matched his.

"You may call me Gideon," he offered. He looked around the room. "Do you clean your own chambers or do the servants hold these rooms as some sort of shrine to the god of cleanliness?"

A smile forced its way through before she could stop it. "I clean them, sir. I cannot live in the squalor that permeates the rest of this house."

His sleepy-eyed gaze settled on her face again. "You are to be commended, I think. Why do you remain here?"

Every question he asked was full of hidden meanings. Just how much did he already know about her? He seemed to be simply waiting for her to admit…something.

"What do you want from me?" she asked with exasperation. Why was she unable to hold onto her composure with this man? She'd known him only hours, knew nothing more about him than his name and his penchant for laziness, and she didn't care a whit what he thought. *That Man* was far more dangerous and she had always managed to avoid letting her feelings show to him.

"I want you to tell me the truth so I know how best to help you. You cannot expect me to guess at this, can you?"

"You seem to know everything. What can I tell you that you do not already know?"

"You can tell me who you work for," he suggested.

"I work for no one."

His pale brows rose slightly. "Then you are taking responsibility for the death of the young man who tried to help you?"

"You can't possibly know… Who are you?"

"I am someone of no consequence. Are you saying his death was your fault or not?" he insisted.

"No consequence? You know every move I make, every word I say before I say it! Who are you?"

Hysteria hovered close to the surface. A few more minutes and they would have every servant in the house breaking down the door to throw him out.

Gideon rose to his feet and knelt by her chair. He took her hand. "I cannot tell you yet exactly who I am, Malvina," he said in a soothing tone. "Trust me when I say I will do everything for you that I can but you have to help me as well. I do not know who is hurting you and that is the vital piece of information I need. Until you give me that, we are at an impasse, I think."

"I don't know," she whispered.

He stared at her for a long moment. "No, you don't," he concluded with a sigh. He stood, staring down at the worn carpet. "Blast. I need his name. What do you call him?" he asked curiously.

"*That Man.*"

He smiled. "I see. Have you never seen him?"

"Not exactly. He visits in the night and stays in the shadows over there." She pointed toward the window seat, which was actually more like a curtained alcove.

Gideon glanced where she pointed. He walked over and looked it over carefully. "When do you next expect him?" he asked, his voice muffled slightly as he stuck his head behind the curtain.

"I never know. Although," she added thoughtfully, "he will probably appear tonight. Since you rode off with me, he will want to be sure I am returned."

Gideon turned to her. "So you are not taking responsibility for that boy's death." It was not a question.

Malvina sighed. "How can I not? I had everything to do with his death even though I did not kill him myself or orchestrate the killing. I blame myself as much as anyone."

Gideon stared at her through carefully expressionless eyes. He said nothing and paced back to his vacant chair. He sat down and leaned back, closing his eyes.

A few minutes passed. Malvina wondered if he had fallen asleep. "Gideon?" she asked tentatively.

His eyes popped open. "So you can say it. I wondered," he said, sleep clouding his voice.

"What are you doing?" she asked, some of her well-cultivated poise reasserting itself.

"Taking a nap, my dear," he murmured with a yawn.

"Why?"

His eyes closed again. "I need to be awake when your friend shows up, so I will sleep now."

She felt her face flame. "You mean to stay the night here?"

"Of course. What did you expect me to do? Leave a message for our villain to meet me somewhere so I can turn him over to the proper authorities? As much as I wish it were that easy, love, it is not."

"But it would not be proper," she protested, ignoring the offhand endearment.

At that, his eyes opened. He stared at her in surprise. "You are involved in the death of a young man, aid a villain in highway robbery, and you worry about impropriety?" He shook his head. "I am amazed that you have lived this long, all alone in the world except for your son, and managed to retain the innocence of an untried girl."

Was that a hint of scorn in his voice?

"And besides that," he added in the same tone, "your reputation was ruined as soon as you told your maid that I was staying."

How could she have possibly forgotten that? She had no reputation now, nor would she ever be able to restore it. Servant gossip was nearly as damning as the truth. Perhaps more so.

3

Malvina lay in her huge bed that night, conscious of the man sound asleep in the chair near the door. She had been surprised when he informed her that he had no intention of making their affair a reality but even more surprising was the curious pang of disappointment she had felt. She was older than him. She should be ashamed of harboring any romantic feelings toward him.

Actually, she was very much ashamed. After so many years with her husband, she really had no use for a man. There had been moments of pleasure in Brackney's arms, but they had been few and not enough to tempt her into an illicit affair with a younger man.

But he was so very handsome. His blond hair curled all over his head in charming disarray and his brown eyes positively danced when he was amused. It was through those eyes that she could tell what he was thinking. He didn't always guard his thoughts or feelings from his eyes. He merely kept his eyelids lowered so only the truly determined were ever successful in divining his thoughts.

She had no business being determined to divine his thoughts, she told herself severely. She snuggled deeper into the feather mattress, trying to compose her mind for sleep.

Unease startled Malvina awake. Her eyes flew open, peering into the lingering darkness. Perhaps she'd had a dream, she thought. She could see nothing in her chamber, but then, it was so very dark that she was unsure she'd know if someone were present.

Something moved near the window. Heart racing with fear, it took but a moment to remember the man who'd rescued her the night before, mere hours earlier. The relief that came on the heels of that memory was incongruent with how little she actually knew about her rescuer. But really, he couldn't be worse than *That Man*, could he?

Regardless of logical arguments against it, she still couldn't help the inordinate relief, the sense of security. It made no sense, but was unlike anything she'd ever felt before.

Her companion paced, his restless energy permeating the room. Earlier, he had seemed like any lazy young man of the *ton*. Now he seemed more like a caged beast, tightly wound, impatient. Anxious.

Daybreak threatened, thin shards of gray light peeking through the shutters. Malvina wouldn't sleep again, her eyes wide open and following Gideon's restless movements. Moments of darkness interspersed with gray dawn as he paced before the window, blocking the light in turns.

She pondered the wisdom of drawing his attention. He seemed much exercised over something and instinct told Malvina it was all about her. He paused, taking a single step away from the meager light, shrouding his body in the dim shadows.

Malvina pushed up onto her elbows, searching the inky shadows for his body but unable to distinguish his form from the shadows around him.

"Awake, are we?"

She nearly jumped out of her skin. "Do not do that!" she said sharply to the dark form who appeared beside her.

She felt rather than saw him smile. "Very well." He stretched out beside her on the bed, linking his hands behind his head. "Your friend is not coming, I think."

"What makes you think that?" she asked, flopping back down on the bed and deciding not to point out the obvious. *That Man* was *not* her friend.

"Word was sent by your servants that I am here, of course," he responded easily. "He is waiting to see which side I am on."

"And which side are you on?" she couldn't help asking.

"Why, yours, dear lady, of course. Why would I be in league with… What did you call him? Oh, yes, *That Man*."

He smiled faintly. "Could you have not invented a more clever moniker for him?"

Malvina's smile was distinctly mocking, though she knew he could not see it. "I felt my tone when I said it to be clever enough, thank you."

"Suitably mocking, to be sure," he told her solemnly.

Her answering snort indicated how much store she put by his words.

Gideon's smile dissipated, his gaze trained on the ceiling above him. Nothing more than pale fingers of light filtered into the room, but still not enough to properly see. He propped himself up on his elbow and gazed at the woman beside him. He could see little more than her outline under the counterpane, not much detail but enough to realize she'd slept fully clothed and that she watched him.

Settling on his back again, he asked, "Why would I be in league with him?"

"Because you are male and very obviously bored with what life has already offered you," she said without hesitation.

Gideon smiled. Malvina Brackney was not afraid to speak her mind. He marveled that a lady as…well, old, for lack of a better word, as she was could remain so completely innocent. She needed a man to take care of her or she'd find herself at the end of a rope.

Well that thought wiped the smile from his face. There was no better way to kill a good mood than the thought of a beautiful woman hanging. And Gideon very much appreciated a beautiful woman. He had to get the bottom of this situation before it was too late.

And he had to get Wolf home before *That Man* decided to punish Malvina for Gideon's rescue.

"You are cynical, my lady," he told her with a yawn. He reached over and lit a candle since it was obvious neither of them would be able to sleep again.

Malvina rolled her eyes at him but refrained from offering any kind of reply. The light from the candle flared in time for Gideon to see her look and he smiled.

Malvina stared at him expectantly for several seconds before she finally asked, "If he is not coming, then why do you stay?"

"Servants." He closed his eyes, trying to distract himself from the lovely woman beside him. Had he been wiser, and less intrigued by resisting his urge to seduce her, he would remove himself from her immediate vicinity.

"Servants?" she repeated. "You are worried about a passel of servants?"

"They believe we are romantically involved. If I leave now, what will they think?"

"This is unbelievable," she muttered. "I am heartily sick and tired of men ordering me about and running my life. Why can't you all just leave me be?"

Gideon ignored this amusing tirade to ask, "When does Wolf come home?"

"He arrives in a fortnight." Was that a hint of a growl in her softly uttered words?

"I will retrieve him in two days," he said, nodding to himself.

"For what reason?"

Gideon's eyes opened at the hint of venom he detected in her voice. "He must be where I can keep account of him. Are you not afraid for him?"

Malvina did not deign to answer this inquiry. "What are you going to tell him? You can't possibly approach him and say, 'Good day. I'm Gideon. I am pretending to be your mother's lover in an attempt to ferret out a government conspiracy. Please don't tell.' He would probably try to call you out or have you arrested."

"Government conspiracy?" He eyed her shrewdly. "What do you know of government conspiracies?"

"Nothing. I was being facetious," she snapped. "Don't change the subject. Wolf is a very volatile young man. I will not have you upsetting him with your tales of killers and intrigue."

"How old is this little firebrand of yours?"

"Sixteen."

Gideon's eyes opened wide. He stared at her in the glowing light of the candle, his disbelief so apparent she felt like slapping him. She knew what his next question would be. "I am two-and-thirty. I was fifteen when Brackney married me," she said on a sigh.

"Fifteen?"

"Just," she breathed, remembering. She stared down at her hands, which were twisting the life out of the coverlet. "Actually, we were married three days after I turned fifteen. Less than one month later, I was expecting Wolf."

Gideon gave her an enigmatic look, his brown eyes intense as they focused on her face. "And you thanked God every day of your marriage that you were delivered of a son," he said suddenly, all signs of boredom gone from his bearing.

"Yes and no," she admitted, blushing faintly. "I was only fifteen, so I was not ready for the intimate side of marriage. I refuse to believe anyone that young is ready. As I grew older, I learned to accept what was what and not to dwell on things I couldn't change." Such as Brackney's penchant for using hurtful words to browbeat his lowly wife into submission. Had he only realized a kind word would have gone much further in gaining her cooperation, their life together would have been much easier.

She released an exasperated breath. "I do not know why I am telling you any of this. It is no concern of yours."

Gideon remained silent for a moment. Then, completely ignoring her statement, he mused, "Wolf will have to get used to the idea that he is about to get a new father."

"*What?*"

He turned his head to look at her. "We will be engaged," he said simply. "He can take no issue with that."

He fell silent. Malvina waited for him to continue but he said nothing. "You must be jesting!" she finally snapped, beside herself and teetering on the edge of losing her temper. "We met *yesterday*! Less than a day ago, and I don't know you beyond your given name."

The look he gave her was vague. "I will be sure to spread the rumor that you have chosen a suitor."

Her temper snapped. "No, sir. We will not pretend an engagement," she uttered in low tones. Had Wolf been present he could have warned Gideon that her quietest tones meant she was beyond incensed.

"Then I tell him I am your lover and he will challenge me to a duel and I will injure him or he will kill me and the bloodshed will be on your head since you are the only one with the power to prevent it." He grinned.

She scowled. "You cannot have thought this through. You are younger than me."

"How do you know that? You do not know me beyond my given name," he taunted.

"How old are you? You appear not more than five-and-twenty."

His grin widened. "I'm not."

Her mouth dropped. "You are younger?"

"No, Lady Brackney. I am seven-and-twenty."

"There, you see?" she smirked. "You are younger and more impulsive. You haven't thought this through. A pretend engagement, indeed."

"You are correct, of course. Although," he said thoughtfully, "I don't think I can really be described as impulsive. Lazy, indolent, a bit of a ne'er-do-well, but impulsive?" He shook his head. "Not impulsive. I tend to think things through very carefully before taking action. For example, I said nothing of our engagement being pretend. It will be real. Hence, the rumors."

"You are crazy," Malvina stated calmly, completely convinced of this fact. "The very idea of an engagement, pretend or real, shows just how impulsive you are."

"I do not know who is terrorizing you and I feel the easiest way to protect you is marriage."

"Engaged is a far cry from married, Sir Bedlamite." She suddenly flew from the bed. "I will not listen to one more word from you. Get out of my house!"

"No."

Malvina was so stunned by this reply, she did not move when he rose from the bed and came to stand over her. She looked up into smoldering brown eyes, eyes that a moment before had been devoid of anything but a certain amount of amusement. She forced herself not to cringe away in fear.

"You, madam, are singularly lacking in sense. Do you not realize I am the only chance you have? If you had any real fear of me, you would have set your servants on me by telling them I am here to see them all transported for their activities. So do not pretend to suddenly realize what a Bedlamite I seem to be just because you are affected by me physically. You are older in years but certainly not sense." He stopped abruptly, straightening. "Never mind. If you want to hang for your part in the murder of that boy who tried to save you, far be it from me to interfere."

Gideon strode from the room, his back rigid.

Malvina stared at the open door, thoughts racing through her head at an alarming rate. Everything he said was true and she knew it. She hated how this man seemed to read her thoughts like a book. But he was the only one who seemed to care a fig about her, however offhanded his concern. He was going out of his way to help her and she treated him as if he was nothing more than a schoolboy out for a lark.

Her stomach sank to her toes. He was gone. Gideon, mysterious man that he was, her only hope, was gone.

Gideon waited just beyond the door, ready to catch her when she realized what a mistake she'd made. He knew she would come to this conclusion since it was the only possible answer.

Despite everything, she was not a stupid woman. Naïve, perhaps, but not stupid.

He had to wonder at his own sanity, however. She was partially right about that. He was not behaving in any kind of rational manner. The truth was, the two kisses he'd shared with her had overset him more than he liked to admit. Something inside him had clicked into place the moment their lips had touched and the thought of life with her had just seemed right.

He didn't believe in love at first sight but he surely believed in attraction. And he was attracted to Lady Malvina Brackney.

He shrugged. He had to marry someday. The succession would perish if he refused.

He saw a flash of dark blue gown from the corner of his eye as Malvina burst from her chamber. Not realizing he was there, she attempted to run past him. Catching her around the waist, he grunted when her body collided with his chest. She gasped.

"Were you looking for me, by any chance?" he drawled with that lazy intonation she was becoming used to.

"I will marry you," she said breathlessly. "That is, if you are still offering."

He favored her with a whimsical grin. "Of course." He released her and, taking her hand, led her back into her bedchamber. He firmly closed the door, turning the key in the lock.

When he turned back to her, his expression grew serious. "You have all the control in this, Malvina. I am completely willing to go through with the wedding. I consider this engagement as real as if I had been escorting you to Almack's for the entire Season with a view to proposing. Think on that until I extricate you from your current situation."

She nodded. "I have one question, though," she said calmly. "Why do we need to be engaged? Can you not simply say you are a friend?"

"That may work with your son but not *That Man*, as you so charmingly call him. If he is someone who knows me, he would know that I would never befriend a woman. Seduction, maybe, but never friendship."

The smoldering look he gave her, the way his eyes swept over her sleep mussed hair and rumpled gown, sent a shaft of desire through her middle. It was a sensation she barely knew, had rarely felt. The flame in her cheeks at that moment could probably vie with her hair for redness.

He sighed and looked over his shoulder, his eyes narrowing. "I wish Hart was here," he murmured to himself. "As vexing as that man is, he is a veritable font of useless knowledge."

"Who is Hart? A friend, I assume."

Gideon shot a sidelong glance at her. "Never assume anything, Malvina. Hart is the Duke of Derringer. No doubt you've heard of him."

"No, should I have?"

"Oh, that's rich!" Gideon laughed. "Hart will be shocked that there exists someone in this world who has not heard of him." Her questioning look grew. "He is famous, my dear. Or, infamous, rather. Legendary, perhaps?"

"What has this to do with anything?" she asked.

"What has anything to do with anything?" he replied. His air of boredom had reasserted itself.

"You, sir, are maddening."

Two days later saw Malvina Brackney swaying along in a carriage on her way to retrieve her son. Gideon sat next to her, staring out the window. She watched him surreptitiously, always with the thought that her life could not have possibly become more complicated. It was difficult for her to believe he was serious about treating the engagement as real. He was, after all, a young and extremely handsome man, born of wealth and privilege.

Two days had certainly allowed her time to learn more of her companion but beyond the information that he was Gideon Mallory, she knew nothing of who he was or where he came from. Every time she asked more pointed questions about his history, he became vague and sleepy, complaining about this or that until she rolled her eyes in disgust and dropped the subject. It was beginning to alarm her.

Perhaps he was the illegitimate son of a prominent Member of Parliament. Although, that would not account for his secrecy unless he was trying to shame his father into acknowledging him. No, it wasn't that. He did not seem the type to engage in such shady dealings, though she wasn't sure how she knew that.

*But what is his real interest in me?* she wondered for the thousandth time just that morning. He could not really want to marry her. He should marry someone young enough to bear him many sons, share his interests, his beliefs, and his upbringing. She was nothing more than the daughter of a Cit, anathema to the upper class.

Although, she supposed she was no longer a member of that class. She had married a baronet, after all, and had had nothing further to do with her family, as was requested by her own father. He'd wanted a member of his family to somehow get in the upper reaches of Society and he had succeeded. To an extent. Brackney had always been ashamed of her, despite her beauty and training as a lady, and had adamantly refused to take her about. She'd never been to London.

It was unfortunate that her father had more or less disowned her. Had he been there for her, to advise her, encourage her, and protect her, perhaps she would not have been dragged into the mess she now faced.

Lord, what was she doing? She was engaged to a complete stranger! That wasn't nearly so bad as her strong desire to actually marry him. She had a feeling life with him would never be dull even though that was the exact persona he tried to convey. Hadn't she already had a few adventures with him, and seen what a vital, tightly wound person was beneath that lazy exterior?

Malvina turned to gaze fully at him and blushed when she saw he watched her. His brown eyes held amusement and his lips curved up just a bit. She looked away, trying to ignore him.

"What is going through that fertile imagination of yours, I wonder," he murmured sleepily. He stretched his legs, still watching her steadily.

Malvina shot him a look of innocence. "Nothing of import, I assure you."

His lips twisted into a full grin. "Indeed? I would hate to call you a liar, my lady, so forgive me if I tell you I don't believe you. You had a far too—frustrated, shall we say?—look on your face for your thoughts to be fleeting."

With a superb effort of will, her expression didn't change.

Gideon shrugged one elegant shoulder. "Very well, I concede your thoughts were pointless. We are arrived, however, and I do think you should at least pretend that we are happily engaged."

A seed of rebellion started in Malvina's mind at his tone. She smiled at him flirtatiously, batting her eyelashes, and parting her lips in a silent invitation, using her powers of observation of the art to show him just how good an actress she was. His look was everything she could have wanted…at first.

She wasn't sure later how or even what exactly happened. One moment she was mocking him with her charade and the next she was in his arms, being thoroughly and expertly kissed. Her head was swimming by the time he released her and when she looked in his eyes, she saw none of his earlier amusement, just a smoldering anger. She drew away from him, alarmed by this other side of him that she had no way of understanding.

"Do not play with fire, my lady," he said harshly. "You will only get burned."

The carriage stopped at that moment, distracting Gideon and giving Malvina a chance to recover her composure. He stepped from the coach and offered her his hand. She placed her hand in his after a brief hesitation.

Upon entering the school, they went to the headmaster's office and were told to wait.

Turning to his intended bride, Gideon requested blankly, "After you introduce me to Dr. Keate as your betrothed, allow me to speak with him alone."

Her face puzzled, she asked, "Why?"

"You must ready your son for the shock he will receive upon meeting me."

Knowing her son better than anyone, Malvina saw the wisdom of this. He would not take kindly to her remarrying and when he discovered it was all a ruse, he would be incensed.

They were taken in to Dr. Keate's office. The man rose when they entered, greeting Lady Brackney a little more warmly than he did Gideon. Neither of his unwelcome guests paid any heed.

"Dr. Keate," Malvina said, offering her hand. "This is my betrothed, Mr. Gideon Mallory."

The headmaster was woodenly polite, clearly not wanting his visitors to linger longer than absolutely necessary. "Is there something in particular you required?"

"Might I see my son?" she asked. "Privately?"

"Indeed, Lady Brackney," the headmaster assured her. "Mr. Gablehouser will show you where you can wait, and then he will fetch Sir Beowulf."

Malvina smiled sweetly at Dr. Keate, nodded to Gideon, and followed the spotty young Mr. Gablehouser from the room.

"Why did Lady Brackney introduce you as Mr. Mallory, Lord Holt?"

Gideon lowered himself into a chair across from the older man. Smiling lazily, he said, "I have not told her who I am."

Dr. Keate's expression became thunderous. "Is this some mad lark? I realize you were a bit of a thoughtless whelp, but I never would have suspected you of such ungentlemanly conduct."

"Indeed?"

Grunting, the headmaster seated himself, the large desk between them. "That reprobate Derringer would have done far worse. I had thought you would be wiser."

"Ah, I have my reasons, sir." He smiled slightly. "Suffice it to say, it is for her safety that I withhold my identity." Straightening slightly, he continued. "What can you tell me about young Brackney?"

Dr. Keate studied Lord Holt for a long moment. Then, he sighed. "I am not sure it would be right to disclose such information with you, my lord. I do not know what game you play and a lady's reputation is involved."

"I am not out to injure her, sir. I seek to help her."

Another long moment passed in which Gideon attempted to remain still, slumped in his chair with his usual air of insouciance. Finally, the headmaster relented.

"He is an average scholar. His studies are affected by his attitude; he does not lack intelligence. He is angry and bitter, taking it out on his fellow students and even some professors. He has been sent down more than once. I suspect it all has something to do with his father."

"There were mysterious circumstances surrounding Brackney's death," Gideon inserted thoughtfully.

"The boy does take umbrage when the late Sir Richard is mentioned."

"Why?"

"I do not care for gossip, mind you, but it does have its uses. It was brought to my attention that some of the other students have been poking fun at Sir Beowulf. Something to do with his father spying for the French. All nonsense, of course, but enough to cause anger in any young man."

Gideon's features remained impassive with an effort. Rumor suggested exactly what the Home Office did. But then, the Home Office wouldn't have known if rumors didn't abound.

"You have given me much to think about, Dr. Keate. I thank you for your candor. It will be a challenge to guide the young man, but knowing what drives him will be of some help."

The headmaster's face became thoughtful. "Are you not younger than Lady Brackney?" he asked.

Gideon released an exasperated sound. "Is this what I am to expect for the rest of my life?" he wondered aloud. "Yes, sir, I am younger. What the devil that has to do with anything, I've yet to discover. The next person to ask me that shall meet me at dawn, I think."

4

"Are you not younger than Mama, sir?"

They were the first words Gideon was greeted with upon seating himself in the carriage. The question was worded innocently enough but the tone contained supreme insolence.

Gideon nearly swore. The red-haired imp of Satan offered a challenge from dark blue eyes. The child was large, broad in shoulder, tall, and muscular though he retained a bit of the lankiness common to adolescence. In all Gideon's musings, he could not have imagined this man-child, this angry behemoth who not only dwarfed his mother, but nearly dwarfed Gideon as well.

Of course, he should have expected this question from Wolf but the lad was sixteen. Surely he knew better than to ask such personal questions of a stranger, even if that stranger was soon to be his stepfather?

He was about to reprimand the boy but Malvina was quicker. "Wolf, apologize at once for your impertinence.

You have not known Mr. Mallory long enough to ask such things."

"My apologies, sir," mumbled Wolf, his sullen expression and mutinous glare giving the lie to his apology.

Gideon could tell the lad didn't like him above half. He hoped the boy knew better than to interfere with things he shouldn't, but a sinking feeling, brought on by memories of his own adolescence, assured Gideon the lad would be a force to be reckoned with.

Especially if there was any truth in what Dr. Keate had told him just as they were joining Malvina.

"A word of warning, Master Gideon," he'd whispered confidentially. "The young master has a bit of a temper. Takes after his father, I've no doubt. He'll come to a bad end, mark my words. Just as his father did."

Gideon had not had a chance to ask the obvious question to this observation. What specifically had Wolf done to warrant such a warning?

As Gideon observed the lad, he saw in his dark blue eyes a spark of rebellion that put him in mind of a cornered animal. He repressed a shiver. Was the boy dangerous? Unbalanced? Did his mother know anything about it?

Surely, if Wolf had done anything truly dangerous, his mother or the headmaster would have done something about it. Wouldn't they?

Malvina was deep in conversation with her son and Gideon could see that she loved him very much. Her pleasure in his company was not feigned simply for the benefit of a stranger. She was truly happy that they were back together.

Gideon studied her face with her beautiful leaf green eyes, pert little nose, and full, sensuous lips. She laughed at something Wolf said, her eyes lighting up with joy, her lips curving upward to reveal even, white teeth. Her beautiful features were made more so by her smile, her joy, her…relief?

Yes, she looked vastly relieved. He realized in that moment how very worried she'd been over the safety of her son. Had the boy been a danger to her or anyone, she would not appear quite so sanguine, would she?

Gideon felt a headache start in the back of his neck. He did not want to ponder it all in that particular moment. He wanted, instead, to study her beautiful face and enjoy her pleasure in being reunited with her child. He didn't want to wonder why something nagged at his conscious mind, something desperately important, possibly life threatening, something buried deep in his subconscious.

He didn't want to think about his assault on her earlier, didn't want to wonder why her actions had made him angry rather than amused, as they should have done. He stifled a groan as his headache worsened, closed his eyes, and leaned his head back against the squabs of the carriage.

"Gideon?" asked Malvina, worry evident in her voice. "Is anything the matter?"

He forced his eyes open and smiled. "Just a slight headache, my dear. Nothing to worry about," he assured her.

Malvina did not look reassured by this answer. "If you say so," she responded. "Perhaps you will feel better after a rest, sir. You have been so preoccupied lately I am worried for your health."

Gideon felt his eyebrows threatening to rise and determinedly held them down. He looked at her blankly then darted a quick look at Wolf. The boy watched them with the same sullen expression in his eyes. He also had a look of interest at their exchange, a look Gideon couldn't like. He wondered what the boy was thinking.

"I thank you for you solicitude, Malvina, but I assure you it will pass in a moment."

"Are you prone to headaches, sir?"

Gideon favored Wolf with one of his blandest looks. "Only when faced with insurmountable trials with no easy solution in view. But, never fear, young man, I will solve this one." His voice held a note of warning and he knew it.

Malvina shook her head in confusion. "To what trial are you referring?"

"Why, becoming a husband and father all in one month," replied Gideon, smiling easily at her. "I've done neither, you see, and have not the faintest notion how to go on."

He heard a grunt from Wolf's direction but when he looked over, the lad was staring out the window. Let him think what he would about the situation he found himself in. It would give Gideon a much-needed glimpse into the child's brain.

And determine how much he was involved in his father's shady dealings.

Gideon had known his relationship with Malvina's son would be hard going. He had no idea how hard. His only experience with children was the few times he'd ever been around those of Sir Adam Prestwich. They were a good deal younger than Wolf, however, and Gideon had never been expected to have more than a trifling conversation with Adam's children.

Of course, Gideon's sister Samantha would be of an age with Wolf. Gideon wasn't sure he wanted to continue that line of thought.

Wolf avoided him for the most part. Partly thankful for that, Gideon didn't mention it to Malvina. But he worried that the boy would always avoid him. And when they were forced together, Wolf insisted on testing Gideon to see how far he'd go to discipline him.

Gideon despised tests.

Within only a few days of their return to Malvina's home, Wolf fell into what would become a pattern.

Gideon was in the book room, which doubled as an office, going over a few things in his mind. So far, he'd made little headway in his search for Malvina's employer. He had the information Derringer had given him before he disappeared but it was only conjecture and Gideon was having trouble attaining proof. And Gideon's top suspect was in the way of being a friend, which made everything all that much more difficult.

Perhaps he should call on him and ask him outright, he thought with a smile. He would lie, of course, and then Gideon would no longer have the element of surprise, but at least something would have been done.

Gideon slouched a little further in his chair. He found he could think better if he was as eased as possible. Today, however, he was having trouble concentrating. Malvina was uppermost in his thoughts, followed closely by her son.

It was her son that really worried him. He had a sinking feeling in his stomach that the boy had been and possibly still was closely involved in his late father's activities.

As if summoned by his thoughts, Wolf strolled into the room. He caught sight of Gideon and eyed him with dislike. Moving around the chair without a word, he strode over to a particular bookshelf.

Gideon reflected that the boy was doomed to have a temper with his red hair. He already topped five-feet-eleven-inches, making him just barely shorter than Gideon. His face and personality fit his nickname, as his smile was decidedly wolfish and he often growled his words instead of simply saying them. One had the feeling he was hiding something of extreme importance every time he smiled.

The boy turned away from the shelf, favoring Gideon with that smile now, his arms folded over his chest. Gideon braced himself. He wasn't going to like was was coming, he was sure.

"Is she your mistress?"

Gideon nearly swore. That particular question was not what he'd been expecting and he was highly tempted to knock the boy down for his impertinence. There was certainly very little that embarrassed the child.

Gideon donned a blank expression. "I don't see how that is any concern of yours."

"It is my concern, *Gideon*," Wolf retorted, making the name sound like an insult. "She is my mother and I love her. I'll not let an impostor like you threaten her happiness."

"Commendable," Gideon mused, rising to his feet, "if I actually believed you, that is. Your love for your mother has an odd way of manifesting itself, in arguments and unspoken accusations that leave her in tears. Every action you've exhibited since I met you seems to indicate you are nothing more than a spoiled miscreant who is upset at the changes in his life, changes he has no control over. She does not seem happy to me so you'll forgive me if I say I don't believe you."

"You don't know anything about it," Wolf snapped, his temper clearly at the breaking point.

"Do I not? I think I know you better than you know yourself and *that* after only a few days. You are spoiled, ill-mannered, rude, disrespectful, and in need of a sound thrashing."

Wolf's temper snapped, surprising Gideon not at all. The young man growled and lunged for him. Gideon stepped to the side at the very last moment and grabbed his arm, twisting it behind him and holding him motionless. The boy growled again and Gideon marveled at how apt was his name.

"I think it is time we came to an understanding, young Wolf," Gideon breathed. He tightened his hold ever so slightly, causing Wolf's muscles to tense in pain. "I allow that you dislike me and that is your choice. I will not, however, tolerate your disrespect for your mother. She has been through much and doesn't need a demon like you to increase her worry. Agreed?"

Wolf remained stubbornly silent for a few seconds, his attitude making Gideon long to throttle him. Then, finally, the lad nodded once.

Gideon released him. "And no more baiting me, please. I find violence of any kind tedious in the extreme, but that doesn't mean I won't thrash you soundly if your actions warrant it."

Wolf stared at him for a long moment, as if debating whether or not to test that theory, then he grunted something indistinct, returned to the shelf by which he'd been standing, grabbed a seemingly random book, and stalked out.

Gideon sighed in relief. It had been difficult to hold the boy and if Wolf had but realized it, he would not have been able to.

Shoving a hand through his hair, further disrupting his blond curls, Gideon pondered this new problem as he paced. If Wolf and he were at constant odds, Malvina would notice. And Gideon truly did not want her to worry about a son she couldn't control. He wanted, in fact, to remove every worry from her shoulders and make her happy. He wanted to love her.

Gideon stopped in his tracks. His eyes widened a bit and he stared at the floor. A frown creased his brow, hands tightening into fists. He felt like punching a wall.

The worst thing that could have happened, had. He was well on his way to falling in love with her.

This was not good.

Malvina sensed a certain restraint when Gideon and Wolf joined her for dinner that evening. They were polite to each other but with a certain coldness on Wolf's part and a reserve on Gideon's that had her contemplating what could have possibly occurred to cause it.

And Wolf was far more polite to her than he'd been since they'd retrieved him from school. He smiled and inquired after her health, something she couldn't recall him ever having done before.

The gentlemen exchanged a look and Malvina's eyes narrowed. Gideon was behind her son's new attitude, then. She hated to think how this came about as she, more than anyone, knew how temperamental Wolf could be. He had always been a troubled lad, his violent starts worsening dramatically after his father's death. She wondered just how much Wolf knew of his father's activities four years ago.

Malvina shook her head, as if to shake away the memories plaguing her. Glancing up, she realized the gentlemen gazed at her expectantly. Had they asked her a question?

To avoid appearing rude, she murmured, "Yes, of course."

A grin split Gideon's face and even Wolf snickered in a rare display of actual mirth. Malvina felt her own lips inching upward as she asked, "I have agreed to something I normally would not even consider. What is it?"

Gideon shot a look at Wolf. Her son stifled a laugh behind his hand.

The elder of the two turned his full attention on her. "Wolf and I thank you for your permission, my love, but we will pass on dressing in skirts, painting our faces, and dancing a jig in front of Carlton House." Her grin became a reality, a laugh even bubbled forth. "Oh," he continued as an afterthought, "the monkey declines, as well."

She couldn't hold it any longer. She laughed until tears ran down her face, marveling at how very good it felt just to laugh. Then, suddenly and without the slightest hint of warning, her tears became anything but happy. She buried her face in her handkerchief, trying vainly to stem the flow, but to no avail. Misery choked her, consumed her, until all she felt was the burning in her lungs as she struggled to draw a breath.

Too much had happened, was still happening. In an effort to protect her son, she allowed herself to get mixed up with a man whose loyalties were suspect. In an effort to protect herself, she allowed herself to become engaged to a man she'd met only hours before. And now, several days later, she experienced a moment of happiness, a moment of joy with her son and her betrothed. Always present in the back of her mind was the inescapable knowledge of her nemesis, *That Man*.

Sniffling, pressing her tiny scrap of a handkerchief to her eyes and then nose, she was dimly aware of a large form hunkering down beside her chair. A hand clasped her arm, offering comfort when she wasn't sure she even deserved it.

"Malvina, love. What ails you?"

Gideon's warm tones washed over her, sending her into a new fit of sobbing. It was some moments before she was able to respond with a choked, "Oh, nothing, everything!"

"Everything?"

Malvina's head lifted, settling on Gideon's warm brown eyes. The warmth was a little less now, as if her statement had hurt him. Perhaps it had. She'd not been thinking of him when she declared everything in her life was wrong.

"I didn't mean you...us, Gideon," she hastened to assure him.

It struck her in that moment that of all the things in her life, Gideon was one that brought her comfort despite how little she knew of him. But it made no sense to trust him, find joy in his presence. And he could certainly find a much more suitable bride in London.

She admitted, "Though I do have certain reservations about that."

Gideon nodded but said nothing, his face carefully neutral.

Malvina sniffed once, then sighed. She found a large handkerchief shoved under her nose and she accepted it gratefully. As she blew her nose and wiped away the proof of her heartache, she pondered what had made her tears turn suddenly sour.

She had not laughed since she was a girl, she realized, well before she was married. After that, there had never been a reason for laughter. Life and her marriage had been difficult, frustrating, and sometimes downright terrifying. Her husband had been demanding and rough, without a sensitive bone in his body. Gideon treated her with respect, gentleness, and kindness. He made her feel beautiful, loved, and…happy.

He made her happy. That was why she had cried so piteously. This man, this young and beautiful man, had the power to make her happy. She didn't deserve it.

She didn't even know who he was or what he wanted with her. He said he would marry her but he couldn't possibly. His age loomed in her mind, an obstacle to any real relationship they could have.

Her thoughts seemed constantly to focus on that fact. Why was she so against it? It concerned Gideon not at all, or so it seemed. But Wolf didn't care for the age difference at all.

She realized her son wasn't in the room. "Where is Wolf?"

"He has gone to allow you time to compose yourself. No doubt he is pacing the floor in the drawing room awaiting your appearance as reassurance."

New tears threatened but Malvina held them back. Her son was not lost to all goodness, then. He was a good boy at heart, and he would grow up to be a good man. If Gideon was there to guide him. Without Gideon...

A tiny smile fluttered on her lips. "Do you think?"

"Sometimes," he replied flippantly. "When it doesn't tax my poor brain too much."

"That is not what I meant, you awful man," she scolded, suppressing a giggle.

Gideon smiled at her, a smile that held a small amount of sadness. He clasped her fingers. "Malvina, we have all had things in our lives that weigh heavily upon our minds. No one is immune to making mistakes. Sometimes, we need someone to help us through the difficult times we put ourselves through. Do you understand?"

She nodded, understanding far better than he could ever know. "I do, Gideon." She gave him a thoughtful look. "You have done something for which you are ashamed?"

It was as if someone flipped a switch inside him. His eyes shuttered, his mouth firmed, his very essence dulling before her wondering gaze. Evidently, she'd touched a sore spot.

He withdrew from her, reaching into his waistcoat pocket and retrieving a small velvet bag. "This is for you," he said, his action screaming of his wish to not discuss whatever pain he held deep within. Malvina wanted to frown at his lack of trust in her when he demanded so very much of that from her, but she forced a smile instead, pretending interest in the bag he held.

She took the offering, opening the little bag and upending its contents into her palm. Delicate silver chain spilled out, covering the pendant within. Malvina gently moved the chain aside. A single flawless pearl, large and creamy white, accented with a golden topaz and one tiny, grass-green peridot, met her wondering gaze. Her trembling fingers brushed over the bauble. For several moments, she couldn't speak past the sudden lump in her throat.

Finally, swallowing hard, she asked, "Why?"

"As my betrothed, you are entitled to a gift to show my regard." At her frown, his lips twitched. "And a lady deserves jewels to complement her beauty." Her brows twitched upward. He leaned close, sending a shiver over her skin as she wondered if he'd kiss her. His fingers caressed her cheek. "There does not exist a jewel worthy of you, love. I can only hope you find this meager offering...charming."

He broke into a grin at his own words. Unable to suppress her answering grin, she plucked the jewel from its satin bed, handing the bag back to her betrothed. She studied it from every angle, choking back the tears gathering at the corners of her eyes. She didn't know if it was the gesture itself or the words that accompanied the gesture that brought on the waterworks this time.

"Here, allow me."

Gideon took it from her nerveless fingers, pulling her to her feet. Standing behind her, he clasped the thing about her throat, allowing the pendant to settle just above her breasts. She shivered as his fingers traced a path of fire over the back of her neck, the sensation lingering even when he moved to stand before her.

Meeting his eyes, she shivered again. Her fingers rose to touch the pendant. "Thank you," she whispered. "It's beautiful."

"There are more elaborate pieces at my estate, family heirlooms, but I thought this one suited you best."

She could not prevent her jaw from dropping. "Family? How did you come to have this now?"

He shrugged. "I'd just retrieved them from the jeweler —annual cleaning—when my superiors called me in and sent me to investigate a widow suspected of treason." Her shock turned to horror at the reminder of his reasons for being there. He didn't allow her to respond. "I dropped the rest at the jeweler but this one was missed, a bit of an afterthought. I'd tucked into my waistcoat pocket and not noticed it until halfway here." Another shrug. "I believe I was meant to give this to you."

"This is—" Her throat closed on the words, the significance of his gesture slamming her in the chest. "I can't possibly accept this!" She grappled for the clasp, desperate to remove the thing and return it to its rightful place.

His large hands closed over hers, pulling her face close to his. "I am giving this to you, Malvina. No matter what happens, this is yours." He redid the clasp but did not release her. "No matter what."

His lips smiled but his eyes held a tinge of sadness, something Malvina didn't quite understand. She heard the sincerity in his tone, though, and nodded her acceptance. He pressed a quick kiss to her upturned lips and stepped back, holding out his hand.

"Shall we join your son?"

Malvina slipped her fingers into his, oddly determined in that moment to marry this man whether she deserved him or not. One day, she would know everything there was to know about him, even if he refused to open up now. She was patient. Hadn't she spent well over ten years of her life with a man just because he was her husband before God?

This would be easy.

About a week after Wolf's homecoming, Malvina received an unexpected, yet expected, visitor.

The weather was still balmy at the peak of the day. Malvina had taken to walking about unescorted in the woods near the house. She used the time to think and as her problems had increased of late, she had much to occupy her mind.

An insect buzzed close to her ear and she waved it away. As her arm came down, she was grabbed from behind. A hand closed over her mouth, stifling her cry of alarm and cutting off her air. Her captor dragged her backwards, into the trees, until they were hidden from the view of any casual passersby.

She struggled against the arm, desperate to escape as her air slowly dwindled, black edging her vision. Then a voice whispered close to her ear, "If you don't scream, my lady, I will release you."

After a brief nod she was released. She stumbled and nearly fell to the ground but her companion reached out and steadied her with a hand under her elbow.

"Where have you been?" she snapped, her eyes probing the shadows in an attempt to make out his features. "I began to think you had decided to leave me out of your plotting."

"Hoping, more like," scoffed the man. "Unfortunately for you, I still have need of you. I will contact you soon about your next assignment."

"Very well," she answered, knowing she had no other choice. What this man held over her head was enough to make her do just about anything he could think to request.

The man glanced around the wooded area with a distracted look on his face. A patch of sunlight lit his face and he stepped out of it, squinting up through the leaves overhead. His brow crinkled.

In that moment of brightness, Malvina caught ordinary features, handsome yet nothing out of the common way, dark brown hair peeking out from beneath his hat. Then he was hidden in shadow again.

"I hear you have a man staying with you. Care to explain that?" His eyes swiveled back to hers, sliding over her face and down to her bosom. He paused there, eyes narrowing. She could only assume he stared at the pendant she'd taken to wearing, the pretty little gift bestowed on her by the very man he wanted to discuss.

Malvina felt an overwhelming urge to kick him in the shin and run away. A childish desire, to be sure, but one she couldn't help but feel. "I am engaged. You may wish me well."

"Indeed?" he replied, his brows raised slightly. "And will he be a problem for you? I would hate to have to remove him from the scene because he put his nose where it doesn't belong."

"He will not be a problem," lied Malvina. She schooled her expression into one of annoyance, trying to cover her desperate hope that Gideon would prove to be just that. But at the same time, she feared for him.

"And who is the lucky man? All I can uncover is a vague description and his abject laziness."

"Does it matter?"

"It does if you want him to survive the night."

She studied him for signs of an empty threat. She was used to such, having lived with a man who was quite fond of empty threats. Finding nothing but dark promise, she capitulated. "He is Gideon Mallory," she told him, giving him the name her betrothed had given the headmaster at Wolf's school.

A look of sheer amazement crossed the man's face. He snorted a laugh that contained hints of genuine amusement. "Did you say Gideon Mallory?"

"Do you know him?" she asked, unable to hide her surprise.

"The question is, my dear lady, do you?"

5

She didn't think. Reaching the house, she inquired after Gideon's whereabouts and went straight for him. She couldn't remember ever being quite so angry. Not even when Brackney had admitted he had a mistress in keeping. This was far worse.

She refused to consider why.

Malvina stormed into the book room and stood, fuming, before the desk. Gideon sat behind it, his face lifted to hers inquiringly.

He rose slowly to his feet. "Malvina? Do you need something?"

She curtsied deeply, mockery in her every movement. "Oh, no, my lord earl. The question is, how may *I* serve *you*?" Then, muffling the scream that pressed at her throat, she stormed right back out.

Gideon stood behind the desk, speechless, for a full fifteen seconds before the shock turned to rage. Only one person could have told her who he was. And that meant she'd been in contact with the knave who threatened her and she didn't tell him. He'd throttle her.

He found her easily enough. All he had to do was follow the sounds of stomping and muffled shrieks. He threw open the door of her bedchamber and strode in, slamming the door behind him. She paused in her furious pacing and looked at him, her pale green eyes shooting daggers. Wisps of deep red hair waved around her face, strands of flame in the late afternoon sun streaming through the window. He moved across the room until he stood directly in front of her.

"Who told you?" he demanded, barely recognizing his own voice. He had never been so completely incensed in his life. It scared him that this woman could do that to him

"Who told me?" she repeated shrilly. "*Who told me?* You lie to me and you have the gall to demand that I tell you who told me?"

"It is a reasonable demand considering I am not well known in this part of the country. I can think of only one person who would know."

Malvina pushed her face closer to his. "You…lied… to…me!" she bit out.

He could see she'd not get past this one point. So he humored her, focusing on the subject she obviously wanted to discuss. "Of course I lied to you. For all I knew, you could be the ringleader behind these holdups and I'd find myself shot in the back for my pains."

"I would never shoot you in the back, you liar. I'd shoot you square in the face so you could see that it was me."

Gideon took a step back and locked his hands behind his back. He was tempted to shake her until her teeth rattled. "That's good to know, I must say," he responded. "I will be sure to keep any and all weapons out of your lovely hands."

She opened her mouth to say something else, but stopped short. "Lovely?" she said.

His eyes settling somewhere on the ceiling, he took one deep breath, forcing calm through his body. "Your moods leave much to be desired." And he turned on his heel and walked out.

She ran after him, catching him just outside her door. "I am not through yelling at you!"

"I am through listening," he retorted. He shook off her restraining arm but she held on like a limpet. "If you do not release me this instant, madam, I swear I'll shake you until your teeth fall out."

Her grip loosened in the face of his obvious anger. It had not occurred to her until that moment that he was as angry as she was. It made her stop and think. He walked away, his back stiff with fury, and disappeared out the front door.

Gideon did not come back for dinner. He didn't come back until the next morning. By that time, Malvina was too worried about him to be angry. She decided to give him a chance to explain his reasons for lying to her.

Her magnanimous decision was met with resistance. Gideon gave her a tired look from behind hooded eyes and mumbled something she didn't quite catch.

"Excuse me?"

They stood in the foyer, in plain view of anyone who happened to pass through. Gideon had just walked in, rumpled and still wearing the clothes he'd had on the previous night. His eyes were dark-rimmed, increasing his usual air of somnolence.

His hands clenched. "I said," he repeated in a long-suffering tone, "that never was a man plagued by such a fool woman." He made his escape before she could retaliate by slapping him.

In truth, Malvina was far too shocked to do anything beyond stare at him open mouthed. Then, as if disbelieving he might actually do her some harm, she followed him up to his room.

She didn't knock. Pushing open the door, she surprised him. He had already started removing his clothes, his hat, coat, waistcoat and shirt laying across his bed. Distraction held her for a moment, her eyes roving over his back, marveling at the smooth perfection of flesh and muscle.

Almost perfection. She caught a glimpse of faint lines near one shoulder before he turned to face her. His smooth chest rose and fell with each breath.

Her husband had been a rather hairy man, hair on his chest, his knuckles, and in his ears. She supposed that could have been attributed to their great difference in age. She shuddered just to think of it. Gazing upon Gideon's smooth flesh caused a tremor in her limbs that she barely recognized.

They stared at each other for a long while. Then, recalling how very upset *she* was, Malvina forgot how upset *he* was. She advanced on him, her fist raised. "I demand an apology, young man!" Inwardly, she cringed but the words were said. She couldn't rescind them now.

He blinked. Other than a slightly quirked eyebrow, his face was completely blank. She wondered for a second if he'd even heard her.

Then, "Young man?" he repeated slowly. A light began to glow in his brown eyes that had her backing toward the door.

He caught her wrist and dragged her forward. "You sound like my mother, Malvina. Is that what you intended? To sound like my mother?"

"You're behaving like a child," she managed to say, a trifle breathlessly. He stood far too close to her for comfort. He smelled of sandalwood and horses, leather, and every other manly thing she couldn't think of at the moment, her mind refusing to settle on just one thing.

"A child? You think me a child?" he asked, his voice a husky whisper. "Do you need proof that I am a man, Malvina?" he threatened. Her name escaped his lips like a caress, silky and smooth, sending a shiver over her skin.

He didn't wait for a reply. He crushed her to him, his mouth seeking and finding hers. He kissed her in fiery anger, awakening an answering fire deep inside her she'd never known existed. It was unexpected, this level of emotion from this man who seemed so unemotional much of the time.

Although she regretted her angry words, she could not regret the result.

In a voice she didn't recognize, she begged him to make love to her. His lips hovered over hers for a moment before she was marched unceremoniously to the door. He opened it, pushed her out, and smiled grimly down at her.

"Do not test me, Malvina. It is the one thing I'll not stand for."

The door slammed and she heard the key turn in the lock. She stood there for several moments, dumbfounded, before she managed to make her feet move away.

Two of the maids stood tittering behind their hands as she passed. It took the greatest effort to prevent the flame that threatened to climb her cheeks.

Gideon heard her retreating footsteps and slumped against the door. Never had he come so close to saying 'to the devil with it.' He wanted her so badly, his body ached. It had taken a supreme effort of will to stop and remove her from the room. Every muscle, every sexual instinct clamored for satisfaction and not just any. He wanted no one but her, the traitorous, lying, conniving little beauty.

She knew, or at least had seen, the man who plagued her.

He'd just walked through the door after a sleepless night spent scouring the countryside in the vain hope that he might find her persecutor. He had failed, of course. His betrothed's willingness to forgive him for his omission so close on the heels of his failure had frayed his temper to the point of violence. He'd had to walk away. He really thought he might have hurt her if she persisted.

If she truly feared her blackmailer, if she truly was being forced to obey him, she would have told Gideon everything she knew about him in the hopes that Gideon could help her.

A tiny voice whispered that she had as little reason to trust him as he had to trust her. He firmly suppressed it.

Dragging himself away from the door, Gideon moved across the room, desirous now of nothing more than sleep.

If he sent for Harper, his valet, he would have at least one other person in the house he could trust, which would go far in relieving much of his anxiety. And his mother could stop worrying about him and his sister Samantha could be reassured that her source of a dowry was not out somewhere getting himself killed.

Hard on the heels of that thought was the uncomfortable reminder that he needed to pay a visit to his estate. He hated going there, had not been there in several months, in fact. Duty demanded that he journey there soon, as Samantha was sixteen. She'd started hinting about wanting a Season, despite her knowledge that she was betrothed and had been since childhood.

Gideon fell back on the bed, eyes closing. He lay like that for at least an hour before he realized he would not sleep. Malvina's betrayal weighed heavily on his mind, causing an unusual bout of insomnia. He had to do something about that woman before she got more poor boys murdered.

There was also the young baronet to worry about.

Sir Beowulf Brackney was a very disturbed young man and Gideon really did not want to have to deal with that. He was barely a dozen years older than Wolf and his experience with young men Wolf's age was precisely nothing.

Gideon groaned. The boy was headed for a bad end, he could see. He was too angry, too self-destructive to handle what life was throwing at him. But what could Gideon do to forestall that?

He sat up, his head clearing. Of course! He could take them with him on his duty visit to his family. If anyone could help Wolf through his anger at the cards life had dealt him, it was Samantha. She had far more on her plate than Wolf could ever dream.

And if Malvina was at Moorview Park under his watchful eye, she couldn't very well get any more unsuspecting young men shot.

Satisfied with his decision, Gideon fell asleep.

His announcement later that night was greeted with surprise, anger, and a certain amount of fear. Wolf shouted that he would not go, Malvina said she couldn't possibly, and Gideon stated firmly that they were all going even if he had to tie them up and drag them there, kicking and screaming.

"You don't understand," insisted Malvina. She cast a worried glance at her son. "Gideon, if I leave, it would look...suspicious."

Wolf gave her a confused look. "Suspicious?"

"Nothing to concern you, dear," she responded automatically.

"Oh, I see," the young man snapped. "Something, no doubt, that I can't hear because I'm too young to understand."

"No, Wolf. It is something that will get you killed if you know," Gideon drawled. "And it has nothing to do with our departure for Yorkshire, I assure you. I owe my family a visit and I should introduce my betrothed to them."

"What has that to do with me?" demanded the young baronet. "I am not the one marrying you."

"Thank God for that," muttered Gideon. "My mother and younger sister would like to meet you, I'm sure. And I really do need to go but I can't be easy knowing you are here alone."

"I can protect us," Wolf stated firmly, angry lines creasing his face. "I am not a complete ninny, you know."

"I never thought that," retorted Gideon, his face taking on that lazy expression that heralded a bout of forgetfulness.

"I want to know about your family," said Malvina. "And we have to discuss your title as well and why you didn't tell us."

"My title? I am the third Earl of Holt. I've held the title since I was two-and-twenty. My mother is still living, my younger sister is sixteen, my elder sister married several years ago and is happily producing little imps of Satan, and I have a worthless cousin who stands to inherit should, heaven forbid, I die without a son. Anything else you'd like to know?"

Wolf stared at him incredulously. "You're an earl?" He looked at his mother. "And you didn't know?"

*Jaimey Grant*

Malvina frowned at him. "Hush now, Wolf. I'll talk to
you later." Then, to Gideon, "I have no other questions, my
lord." She rose to her feet. "I will retire now. Wolf, attend
me in my rooms."

The boy rose as well, his face a sullen mask of
annoyance. Gideon, annoyed himself, stood, saying, "We
leave at first light, my lady. Be ready."

6

Malvina fretted and fumed, wearing a path in her chamber floor. This was not going to be easily accepted by *That Man*. She finally decided there was nothing left for it but to try to contact him and let him know. If she did not, she knew he would let just a tiny piece of information slip into the gossip mill and, if not get her hanged, see her socially ruined at least.

A shiver ran down her spine as she stole from her rooms and traversed the empty corridors of the home that had been hers since she was fifteen. The servants had gone to bed, the kitchen deserted. She paused long enough to whip a cloak about her shoulders. It still amazed her how cold it could get at night when just the afternoon before had been almost too warm for comfort. With a note clutched tightly in her hand, Malvina opened the kitchen door and walked out into the night.

Her body froze to the spot. Rain came down in sheets, casting a blurry haze over everything in sight. She could wait, she supposed, hope it cleared up before too long. But the urgency of her errand would not allow it. Ducking her head against the onslaught, she made her way to the stables.

The stables were quiet but she could hear the sounds of talking in the back where the head groom lived and overhead where the stable hands slept. She supposed they had just gone up to bed, since their work took them well into the night.

The head groom was a burly man with a perpetual sneer on his ruddy face. He stood well over six inches taller than Malvina, but that was nothing out of the ordinary for a woman of her stature. He waited by the door with a menacing look on his face. He did not appear happy to see her.

Throwing back her hood, Malvina ignored the cold rain sliding down her neck and drew herself up to her full height. "I assume, Halder, that you can get in touch with your master." She took his answering grunt as confirmation and handed over her letter. "Take this to him, please. It is urgent."

He grunted again and took the note, shutting the door in her face.

Malvina stood there for a second, debating the wisdom of what she'd just done. If Gideon found out, he'd assume she was a willing participant in the robberies. He may forget about helping her and just turn her over as the criminal she was. A shudder racked her body, making her pull her cloak tighter. She should not have sent that note, she realized. It was only a matter of time before Gideon found out. How could she possibly explain her actions?

Then there was Wolf. She had tried to explain the circumstances to him without upsetting him or provoking his nasty temper. It hadn't worked and the most frightening part was that she didn't know exactly whom his anger was directed at: Gideon for his secretive part in a mystery even she didn't understand, her part for submitting to a blackmailer, or the man who was daring enough to blackmail her.

She hadn't wanted to tell Wolf the whole truth but the boy had always had a foul disposition and, quite frankly, at times she was afraid of him. So she'd poured it all out to him including Gideon's part. Now, shame filled her, shame at feeling such fear that she couldn't manage to keep the darkness from her child, and shame that with all she'd told him, she neglected to tell him that her feelings for the dishonest earl were becoming far stronger than she could have anticipated. But something had held her back from disclosing this realization and now she had her child's anger to contend with because he believed she was being put upon by two different importuning men. His loyalty did him credit but his fierce temper was a decided drawback.

Malvina retraced her steps into the house, her thoughts and the drenching rain making her far less observant than was her wont. So it was no wonder, then, that she failed to see the man leaning negligently against the kitchen door, hat pulled low against the rain.

"Where are you bound, Malvina?"

She jumped, heart fluttering against her ribs. "Gideon! Whatever are you about scaring a body like that?"

"If you were not wandering around outside at night with a lunatic band of highwaymen on the loose you would have no need to be frightened," he remarked. "What were you doing?"

His face remained in shadow and she could detect nothing from his voice. The flutters in her chest became thunder. "I needed a breath of fresh air," she said, her voice sounding unconvincing to her own ears. She had to remind herself to take a breath and fight the wave of guilt that threatened to color her voice.

"And Halder was helping you breathe?"

Malvina cast a nervous glance in the direction of the stables, but she refrained from turning her head, hoping her companion wouldn't notice her hesitation. "Halder? What are you implying?"

"Or," he suggested, "perhaps he knew of the best air to breathe and you were merely asking his advice."

"No, I—I was merely— He wanted to tell me something and I…"

Her voice trailed off into nothingness as he pushed away from the wall and approached. He loomed over her, his next words deadly level, intensely quiet. "And did the head groom give you his message, Lady Brackney?"

She nodded, her unease not allowing her to answer in any other way. She didn't dare tell him there was no message, that she was the one sending missives.

"I see. And what was the message, Malvina?"

"I don't remember," she told him weakly, desperate to get away before she stupidly revealed her real purpose in wandering the grounds in the rain. "I must go in, Gideon. It is quite chill out here"—she glanced up, blinking against the rain—"and I am tired."

Gideon stopped her from retreating by simply stepping in front of her every time she tried to go around him. The third time she ignored him, he took her firmly by the shoulders and gave her a little shake.

"Malvina Brackney, you will not walk away from me until you explain yourself. If you continue to fabricate excuses for your presence outside in the middle of the night, I'll begin to think you are having an affair with a groom."

Malvina glanced up into his darkened face. "I am not having an affair with a groom," she soothed. "And I do not appreciate being thought a liar simply because I do not wish to tell you my business. If anyone is a liar, *Gideon Mallory*, it is you!"

He laughed, the unexpected sound sending a shiver over her skin. "My name truly is Gideon Mallory," he told her. "Well, two of my names."

Distracted, she asked, "Who are you? I mean, truly? Who sent you to find me? Why are you here?"

He sighed and dropped his hands to his sides. "It is perhaps a bit too wet out here for this discussion, do you not think?"

He ushered her inside and up to the drawing room where a fire smoldered in the grate. Stooping, he worked the embers into a good blaze, speaking as he prodded at the wood.

"I was born in Yorkshire and raised on my father's estate, Moorview Park. I have an elder sister who married very young—fourteen, I think—so I was essentially the only child until I was eleven. Then Sammy was born." He stopped working on the fire and rose to his feet, turning at the same time.

Malvina lingered near the door, as if she'd flee at the slightest provocation. He sighed and motioned her to a chair. She sat while he paced the chamber, talking, his mind caught up in bittersweet memories.

"Sammy, Samantha, that is, was a beauty from the day she was born. As she grew older, she was the envy of every young girl in the village of Holt. Even Stokesley had nothing to compare to her beauty. Then father died. Sammy wasn't even thirteen yet, and I was twenty-two.

His death affected us greatly, my mother especially. She became a shell of her former self. In spite of her young age, Sammy has been the one to hold the family together.

"But that really has nothing to do with it. I want you to know what they are like so you are not surprised when we go there. My mother will not like you simply because she hates change and my marriage would be a great change. Sammy loves everybody though she is a bit more... reserved... now."

He paused, looking back to his past, his brown eyes glowing with what looked like pain. It was quickly gone, however, and Malvina felt that perhaps she'd imagined it.

"My grandfather was the first earl," he continued suddenly, "having received his title from King George for an undisclosed piece of government work. Even my father didn't know what it was. I have always wondered myself but all family records make no mention of it." He shrugged, falling silent.

Malvina had just decided he was done talking when he added, in an offhand manner totally at odds with the import of his words, "Sammy is horribly disfigured. There was a mishap several years ago and her face and hands were badly burned."

Shock was too mild a word to describe the feeling that went through Malvina at this disclosure. "Is she all right? Is she in any pain?"

"I suppose she must be," he replied thoughtfully, staring into the leaping flames in the fireplace. "She was burned over the left side of her face, both hands, and her chest."

"How did it happen?"

Gideon swung around and looked at her. His eyes shuttered, his face closed, and she knew they were done talking for tonight. "A mishap," he repeated, his look telling her accurately that she would not find out any time soon.

She rose and gave him a tired little smile. "Good night, Lord Holt."

As she walked to the door, his next words stopped her, freezing her blood.

"Mark my words well, Lady Malvina Brackney. I will know your purpose in the stables this night. Pray to God I am not displeased with what I find."

7

The young baronet sat in brooding silence for the majority of their long journey to Yorkshire. Gideon wondered what was going on in his head and then decided he'd rather not know. The boy would soon be under Samantha's control. Even with the scarring, she was still a very beautiful girl and full of life. He admired her but he avoided her as much as possible.

Gideon shoved his mind away from his sister and focused on his newest problem. Malvina. He had had the devil of a time when he questioned the head groom. The task was made more difficult by the fact that he'd had to be as vague as possible to avoid alerting the man to his real purpose. It had gotten him exactly nowhere.

"When will we arrive, my lord?" Malvina asked days later.

She had a vague, questioning look on her face that indicated how she was distancing herself from him and the entire situation in which she found herself. Gideon told himself he was pleased.

He stared out the window as if something in the passing scenery would tell him. Then, in as offhand a tone as he could affect, he replied, "As it is a distance of well over one hundred and seventy-five miles, the entire journey will take a few days at least, my lady. And as we have already been traveling for just over three days, I suppose we will arrive at Moorview Park presently."

"Well, that would explain why you are unknown in Gloucester," muttered Malvina, her tone just barely civil.

Gideon gave her a long look from beneath hooded lids. "You are correct, of course. Though, I should point out, I spend most of my time in London. I haven't visited in many months."

"Why not?" asked Wolf, betraying he had at least a modicum of interest in what was going on.

Gideon smiled. "Personal reasons."

The young baronet resumed his silent appraisal of the passing countryside. Malvina pursed her lips and stared moodily out the other window. Gideon had to repress a smile of amusement.

His amusement was swiftly killed when Wolf looked at him and said, "This is kidnapping, you know."

"Excuse me?"

"Did I stutter? Or do you just not understand the King's English?" queried the boy nastily, ignoring the warning pinch from his mother. "I told you, my lord earl, that you are kidnapping us. It is still illegal, I'm sure, even for a peer."

"Indeed it is," agreed Gideon easily enough. His brown eyes met Wolf's blue ones. "Unfortunately for you, young Master Beowulf, I am not kidnapping you."

"Just because you're not forcing my mother to do horrible things in exchange for your silence does not make you any better than that other scoundrel!" Wolf snapped, beside himself with rage. A look of suspicious horror crossed his young face as a sudden thought occurred to him. "Or are you? Do you take your payment from her body?"

"Wolf!" Malvina's face heated at her son's scandalous suggestion. "Please!"

"What, Mother? Do you want me to apologize to him for what he's done? Do you think he deserves it, the way he's been treating you? And what about my accusation? Look at how he sits there with that stupid smile on his face as if he has not a care in the world beyond exploiting you. What of it?" he demanded, his gaze locking with Gideon's.

Gideon had his temper under tight rein. He wanted nothing more than to soundly thrash the boy for suggesting such a thing of an honorable man and having the bad manners to do so in front of his mother. He glanced out the window, noting with relief the line of rowans that heralded the border of his estate. For the first time since Sammy's mishap, he was glad to be home.

"We've arrived," he announced as the coach turned between two large oak trees flanking the drive. He eyed them both impassively. "If I had anything to be ashamed of, I assure you, I'd leap to my own defense since both actions are that of a dishonorable man."

The carriage fell into an uncomfortable silence, each occupant mulling over different things. Gideon noticed the death-like grip Malvina had on her son and he wondered if perhaps the lad was itching to attack him. What made the young baronet so angry, in general?

Something flashed by, catching Gideon's eye. His sharp gaze caught the tail end of a horse and rider as they shot through a field located a few hundred feet from the house. He supposed it was Sammy, out taking her usual afternoon run on Goldenrod.

The incident was pushed from his mind when the carriage drew to a halt. The steps were let down, the door opened, and Malvina was helped from the conveyance by one of the earl's own servants. Gideon climbed down after Wolf, and stood looking at his childhood home with the same weary feeling of bittersweet memories he'd always experienced. It was a lowering thought to realize it may always be so.

Offering Malvina his arm, he said, "Shall we? I am sure Mother received my message and has prepared for our arrival."

The servant who'd assisted them signaled the earl a trifle nervously.

"Yes, Samuel, what is it?" asked Gideon, smiling.

His smile was impatient and the servant, a fairly new one who did not know the earl very well at all, took a huge breath and said, "Welcome home, my lord."

One brow quirked and Gideon's smile became genuine. "Thank you, Samuel. It is good to be back."

The servant bowed and shuffled off for the Lord only knew where.

Gideon, who watched the servant depart with a look of serious thought upon his face was abruptly brought back to the present when Malvina tugged gently on his arm.

"My lord? Are we to stand out here all afternoon? I must confess to being a good bit tired after such a long journey."

"Yes, of course." He led them up the wide stone steps to the front doors, which were standing open with Keeley, the aging butler, wringing his hands in obvious agitation.

The earl's brow furrowed. "Keeley, whatever has you in such a pother?" he asked with all the informality of one who'd had many of the same servants since birth.

"Oh, Master Gideon, I am that upset, I am," the family retainer uttered in a distressed whisper. "Her ladyship, your good and kind mother, has ordered that certain rooms be made up for your guests and I cannot bring myself to do so. It would be the height of rudeness and I know it would displease you immensely. But I cannot simply tell my mistress that I will do no such thing, my lord, I cannot. I like to think I am far better trained than that."

"Indeed, you are, my good man. And which rooms has my mother deemed worthy of my future wife?"

"*The* rooms, my lord," replied the butler in a tone of foreboding.

Gideon frowned. "What was she thinking? She knows how depressing those rooms are. Anyone staying in them would take to their heels within moments of setting foot in them... Ah, I begin to understand." He turned to Malvina. "It seems my mother's reception of you might be even chillier than I expected. I apologize in advance."

Malvina, who heard this entire exchange with mingled astonishment and confusion, did nothing more than nod her acceptance. What else could she do? If she refused to meet his mother it would make for a most uncomfortable two weeks.

Wolf was more inclined to voice his opinion. "Why should she not like Mother?" he demanded.

"It is nothing personal, I assure you," replied Gideon, neglecting to add more.

A trim little figure of equestrienne superiority erupted into the house. She twirled her shako hat on one finger, her smile of utter delight encompassing all those assembled in the great entry hall.

This was Gideon's sister, Malvina realized. The way she carried herself would have been indication enough but the rippling scars covering the young lady's cheek confirmed her identity.

Malvina was intrigued to note the disappearance of the charming smile as the young lady's eyes lit upon the earl. Indeed, it was as though the light in her had been extinguished. They were suddenly faced with the epitome of a well-bred English lady.

"Hello, Holt. I hope your journey was without mishap?"

Her voice carried a distant note that was not lost upon Malvina and her son. Lady Brackney gave the earl a questioning look that he ignored and she had to pinch Wolf before he said something embarrassing, like mentioning the young girl's scars.

"Our journey was uneventful, was it not, my dear?" he said in reply to his sister's question. His brown eyes settled on Malvina, awaiting her agreement.

"Very pleasant," she murmured.

"Sammy, love, this is my betrothed, Lady Malvina Brackney, and this is her son, Sir Beowulf. My sister, Lady Samantha de Witt."

Samantha curtsied politely, smiling at his companions in an unselfconscious way that Malvina found curious.

"Where is Mother?" Gideon asked.

Samantha looked up at him. "She has sequestered herself in her apartments, Giddy."

Malvina's lips quirked. What an oddly disarming pet name, she thought. It didn't suit the earl in the least.

His response was unaccustomedly curt. "Why the devil has she done that?"

The girl threw an uncertain look at Malvina, telling that lady succinctly that it was all her fault and Samantha did not want to seem rude by saying it aloud.

"Oh, the old bat doesn't want us here," blurted Wolf in a particularly abhorrent display of bad manners. "That's easily solved. Mama, we will leave."

"Wolf!" said Gideon and Malvina together, both thoroughly exasperated with him.

"Oh my," murmured Samantha, her eyes round with wonder as she took in the monstrous splendor that was Sir Beowulf Brackney. "You are something, are you not?"

Wolf seemed unsure how to take her remark. He gave her a rather odd look, frowned, then snapped, "What happened to your face?"

A faint tinge of pink appeared on her cheeks, the rippled scars standing out in stark relief against the unmarred portion of her face. "A mishap," she replied, giving her brother a quick glance that no one seemed to understand but that particular man.

"You don't truly want to leave, do you?" she asked suddenly, returning her gaze to the young baronet. "I mean, it is rather lonely being the only young person here and I would really appreciate the company. Do you ride?"

"Of course I do," he snapped. "Everyone does."

"Not everyone," contradicted Lady Samantha. "My mama doesn't and my governess, Miss Pymm, doesn't, either. They are both afraid of the horses."

"But they're *females*," retorted Wolf, as if he had just uttered the most dreadful of insults. "All men ride."

"Perhaps you can take Wolf out to the stables so he can select a mount to use while he is here," suggested Gideon.

Wolf reluctantly left with Lady Samantha. Gideon ushered Malvina into a small morning room just off the front hall and closed the door. He turned to her and smiled in a rather self-deprecating fashion. "I realize it is not proper for us to be closeted alone together like this, and if Mother knew, she'd be inconsolable, but I feel the need for private conversation with you."

"Very well, my lord. What is it you wish to say to me?" She felt cornered and was unsure why.

"I only wish to apologize on behalf of my mother, Malvina. Please don't take her actions to heart." His easy smile slipped into place, reassuring her far more than it should have.

"I shan't," she replied, allowing the smallest smile in response. She looked away and bit her lip. Then, she asked, "Why did you send Wolf out with your sister? I am afraid he will treat her dreadfully. I do not know where I went wrong with that boy but never have I witnessed such blatant rudeness as he's displayed since he joined us. I apologize for him, my lord."

"I imagine it has nothing to do with you or I at all," he responded. "There is something in that boy, something dark and angry that finds its only outlet in bad manners. That doesn't mean, of course, that he is necessarily bad, simply…angry. I wonder why."

"As do I," murmured Malvina thoughtfully. "He started acting this way just after Brackney died. He lashed out every time his father was even mentioned. It has never been quite this bad before, however."

Gideon studied her face closely. "I see," he finally replied, his expression enigmatic. Then, magically, his easy smile returned and he added, "As for my sister, I think you will find that Sammy can hold her own with the fiercest of tempers."

8

Days later, Malvina had reason to believe Gideon's claim that Samantha could indeed hold her own. In fact, the young lady seemed to have wrought a miraculous change in Wolf. He smiled more, treated everyone he came across with respect and courtesy, and was just overall a far more pleasant person to be around.

There was one incident that caused a bit of a setback, however.

A few days after their arrival in Yorkshire, they were granted an audience with Lady Holt. Malvina viewed this meeting as a particularly painful form of torture and to judge by the long faces of Gideon and Wolf, they viewed it the same. The sight of them wearing the same expression would have elicited a grin from Malvina had her own nerves not been bound so tight.

Early in the afternoon, they were ushered into a darkened room. Malvina could just barely make out the very small figure of a woman reclining on a chaise lounge by the fireplace. A blanket was thrown over her knees and a small table next to her was littered with bottles of tonics and packets of powders.

Malvina turned shocked eyes on her betrothed. "Is your mother an invalid, sir?" she whispered.

"No, my dear, she is not," he responded grimly. Louder, he said, "Mother, how are you this afternoon?"

"Lower your voice, please, Holt," complained the countess. "My head aches abominably, and you are the cause, you dreadful boy."

"Thank you, Mother," he replied dryly. His whole face brightened. "Since you are unwell, Mother, we will go."

"No, child, I want to get this meeting over with," she retorted plaintively. "Have you brought the encroaching mushroom? I understand she has a rather unsavory reputation and a horrible son to go with it."

"Mother," he said in a warning tone that Malvina had only heard once before. She shivered at the memory.

"Well bring them forward, Holt, do. You will be the death of me yet."

Gideon leaned closer to Malvina. "I wish I could spare you this ordeal, love, but it will happen someday, you know."

Malvina had her doubts, but she stayed silent on that score and moved forward with him, her son trailing behind sullenly.

"Mother, I'd like you to meet Lady Malvina and her son Sir Beowulf Brackney."

The tiny lady glanced up with a look that closely resembled Wolf's. Malvina smiled warmly and offered her hand. The woman regarded it like a repellent species of insect, sniffed haughtily, and turned her head away in a clear snub.

Gideon released an audible growl of annoyance at his mother's display of rudeness. He opened his mouth, no doubt to reprimand her, but she spoke first.

"Such dreadful names," she murmured nastily, "indicate persons of weak character." Her gaze turned once again to Malvina, who stood in embarrassed silence. "Perhaps even low moral character."

Wolf's face darkened ominously. Gideon and Malvina saw it at the same time and both tried valiantly to stop the young man but failed. He took a step closer and leaned down, pushing his face up next to Lady Holt's.

"Listen to me, you miserable old bat. If you dare to imply that my mother is a whore, I will make you sorry. And believe me when I say that I do not make idle threats."

His voice carried a deadly menace that Malvina had never heard before and she wondered for the first time if perhaps her son was truly evil.

"Holt, remove this person from my presence," gasped Lady Holt.

"Wolf, come," ordered Malvina.

"Not until the bat apologizes," he insisted stubbornly.

Gideon snapped his fingers and a hovering servant approached, her face carefully blanked of all expression. He whispered a few words to her and she practically ran from the room.

He then returned his attention to the furious baronet. "I agree that my mother's behavior is disgraceful, Wolf, but I will not tolerate any insult toward her."

"I don't care," Wolf bit out. "Nobody calls my mother a whore."

"Except you?" asked Malvina softly.

Wolf's face flushed a bit, and then he looked down at his feet and muttered something no one caught. Looking up, he said more clearly, "I was angry still, Mama. I never really believed you were…you know."

The door opened, yielding the breathless servant who'd just left, followed by Lady Samantha. She crossed the room with a look of question on her young face. Her gaze settled on Wolf, who gave her a look of surprise.

"What are you doing here?" he asked.

"I am here to prevent a murder, it seems," she replied, not even the hint of a smile tugging at her lips. "Tell me what has happened."

To everyone's considerable shock, Wolf obeyed. Even Lady Holt remained silent, her face registering her own surprise at the budding friendship between her kind-spirited daughter and the volatile young man.

"It appears, Wolf, that you owe Mother an apology," concluded Samantha.

"Why is that?" he demanded sharply. "She insulted my mother."

"You didn't let me finish," the girl admonished gently. Her gaze fell on her mother. "Mother, you really oughtn't have said something so completely dreadful. You do owe Lady Malvina an apology, as well."

"Not until he apologizes," she muttered stubbornly.

Wolf rolled his eyes heavenward. "Very well! I apologize for frightening you, Lady Holt, and I most humbly beg your pardon."

"Well, I don't accept it," snapped her ladyship. Her gaze went again to her son. "Throw him out, Holt. I do not want this person in my house."

"Well, then, Mother, it is a good thing this is not your house," retorted Gideon, clearly at the end of his patience.

"Oh! How can you speak to me like that?" she said, beginning to sob. "If your father were alive he'd take a whip to you for your impertinence."

"Mother," inserted Samantha with perfect calm, "you know very well Father would have done no such thing." She shot a glance at her brother, rife with meaning.

"He would," Lady Holt insisted.

Samantha crouched beside her mother, lowering her voice though it still carried to Malvina's ears. "He did once, but you know why that happened."

"Yes, dear, your poor face," the countess murmured, sniffing back tears. "You would have done so well in London, too. Such a shame."

Gideon tensed. All along his arm, where Malvina's hand had rested comfortably, his muscles hardened until it felt like she was grasping a stone. She stared up at him, dimly aware that her son stared as well.

They were thinking the same thing. How was Samantha's mishap Gideon's fault?

Watching the internal struggle manifest itself in his brown eyes, Malvina was not surprised when his customary lazy grin appeared.

"Shall we allow Mother to rest?"

Dinner that evening was conducted with the utmost formality, a circumstance Malvina found tedious and dull. Lady Samantha and Wolf kept up a steady flow of conversation while Lady Holt stared moodily at her plate. Gideon wasn't even present and Malvina wondered why the countess had felt it necessary to venture from the seclusion of her chambers to join them.

Dinner finally ended and Malvina was inordinately relieved when the countess stated that she was too fatigued to join them in the drawing room.

Wolf followed the ladies as he had no desire to sit over a glass of port by himself and he had not yet taken up the habit of smoking. They made no demure when he apprised them of this and seemed to welcome him wholeheartedly to join them in the drawing room.

Samantha offered to entertain them on the piano. Malvina was absolutely delighted as she had no talent herself for the instrument but loved to hear it played. Wolf gallantly offered to turn the pages for her.

"That it not necessary, Wolf," she replied. "I do not use music sheets, merely playing from memory." At the fallen expression on the young baronet's face, she relented somewhat. "I would love it, however, if you would sit here, as a sort of…support."

Wolf eagerly agreed and Malvina had a feeling he was forming a *tendre* for the beautiful Lady Samantha despite her physical deformities.

To their considerable surprise, she launched into an intricate sonata by the composer Scarlatti. Her fingers fairly flew across the keys and she never made a mistake. Wolf sat in dumbfounded silence, as did his mother, until the girl finished. She blushed at their open mouthed expressions. They broke into praise at the same time and she blushed again, making her scars stand out alarmingly.

Malvina requested another song and Samantha played a more subdued Mozart concerto. They were at ease and enjoying the music when Malvina felt another presence in the room. She looked toward the door to see Gideon standing there, his face unreadable. Their eyes met and he gave her a warm smile, one that made her insides feel like a jelly.

Samantha finished with a flourish, her hands poised above the keys. She hit the final chords and eased the tension in her body.

Steady clapping came from the door and the young people on the piano bench turned as one to look. Gideon strode into the room and lowered his tall form into the seat next to Malvina. She stared at him in wonder, noting the rather careworn look that had come to reside on his handsome face since their arrival in Yorkshire. His brown eyes seemed infinitely tired and his mouth tended to droop at the corners. He was not happy to be home. Tension surrounded him like a cloak, keeping everyone else at a distance.

Simply the cares of managing an estate?

Samantha gave her brother a long, blank look. Then, she returned her attention to the ivory keys in front of her and started playing again. This time the song was melancholy with a deeply haunting melody that tore at one's soul. Malvina did not recognize the composer. It was unlike any of the composers with whom she was familiar, but then, her knowledge of music was somewhat limited.

Samantha finished on a low note. Malvina clapped, saying, "That was lovely! Who is the composer?" She released an embarrassed laugh and admitted, "My knowledge of music does not compare to yours, I fear."

Samantha didn't answer. She gave her brother a steady look, one that lasted so long Malvina began to wonder if anyone would answer.

A moment later, Gideon informed them flatly, "It was composed by someone of no account whatsoever."

Samantha gave Gideon a look of complete disgust before turning her attention back to the piano. She pounded out Mozart's eleventh sonata with great verve, slamming the keys so hard at the end that the entire house seemed to vibrate with the crashing of the instrument. Malvina stared at the girl in concern, for surely this was unusual behavior? She glance at Gideon, wondering why he did not put a stop to Samantha's abuse of the piano and was surprised by the banked anger burning in his eyes. His lips smiled grimly and he clenched his hands in his lap. What transpired here?

"Very good, Sam," remarked Gideon. The biting sarcasm in his tone was not lost upon anybody. "Perhaps your next amazing feat can be tuning the piano."

Samantha turned fully around on the piano bench to glare at him. "Oh, stubble it, Giddy, do!" Her fingers gripped the edge of the bench, white knuckles attesting to her upset. "You always come home, feeling sorry for yourself. Why is your life so distressing? Did the government ask you again to kill your friend?"

She stood and took a deep, calming breath, smoothing her hands over her pale skirts. Moving to stand next to her brother, she looked down at him. When she spoke, her voice was just barely above a whisper.

"Nothing is ever your fault, Giddy. I wish you would stop believing that it is your job to fix everything. Some things cannot be fixed." She sighed and looked away. "Indeed, perhaps some things are better left the way they are."

Lady Samantha left the room with as much dignity as a queen. Wolf stood, following her out without so much as excusing himself. His rudeness was the least of Malvina's current worries.

Gideon sat so still beside her that Malvina wondered if he'd fallen asleep.

"Gideon?"

"Go to bed, my lady," he said dully.

"Gideon, I—"

"Go to bed, Lady Malvina."

Malvina stood hesitantly, not wanting to leave him in such an odd state. "Gideon, let me—"

He looked directly at her, dark gold eyes flashing with anger, annoyance, and...something else.

"Go to bed, Malvina, or I will take you to bed," he threatened in a soft tone that promised dire consequences should she refuse.

It was then she understood the glint in his eyes. His upset could quickly translate into some other emotion entirely if she tested his patience. It was not to her own bed he would take her.

Something thrilling shot through her body. Part of her wanted very much to test him, wanted to find out what it would be like to be with him. But the other half, the sensible half, was scared out of her wits by the deadly threat in his tone and wanted nothing more than escape. She paid heed to her sensible side and fled his overwhelming presence.

Gideon sat in brooding silence for nearly an hour. He stared at the piano where Samantha had recently played her heart out and wondered what had come over him to make such a hurtful remark.

He supposed it was all spurred by guilt. No matter what his sister believed, it was his fault that she was so horribly scarred. If he and his friend, Trent, had not been conducting experiments with sulphuric acid, she would never have mistaken it for plain water.

He leaned forward, covering his face in his hands. Dearest God in heaven, she was only eight when it happened!

His stupidity had robbed her of her beauty, a stunning loveliness that was already apparent at such a tender age. If Trent hadn't been there to pull her away...

Gideon shuddered. It could have killed her. After days of fever and sickness, the child had finally recovered, the healing scars a constant reminder of exactly how careless he'd been. He'd never spoken to Trent again, but that was something he'd have to right very soon. Trent's part in the mishap carried consequences of a different sort. He'd betrothed himself to Samantha, promising to marry her when she came of age. It was the least he could do, he'd said, considering it was through their negligence that she'd be unlikely to contract a suitable alliance.

Standing, Gideon paced over to the pianoforte and sat down, running his hands over the keys. His fingers found the notes just recently played by his sister, the melancholy tune that had so moved Lady Malvina Brackney.

It was a piece he knew from memory. It was unnamed, composed by an amateur who had much time on his hands and much sorrow in his heart.

Gideon wondered if it accurately told Samantha how very sorry he was for hurting her.

9

It was three days later, nearly one week into her visit to Moorview Park, just when she thought perhaps he had forgotten her or decided it would no longer do to blackmail her, that Malvina received word from *That Man*.

She sat in the drawing room, unusually alone, when one of Gideon's many minions entered to inform her that there was a gentleman asking to see her in the gardens. Taken completely by surprise at such a request, Malvina consented to meet the gentleman and followed the servant out.

Just as the servant turned to leave, she asked, "Has my lord been informed?"

The girl shook her head. "No, milady. *He* asked that no one else be told," she replied with a curtsy.

Malvina frowned as she wended her way to the gardens at the rear of the house. Who on earth would...?

"My dear Lady Malvina, I'd begun to despair of your ever leaving the house."

Malvina turned slowly, schooling her features into an expression of blank inquiry. "Sir? I assure you, I have not kept solely to the house. I have no reason to hide, after all."

They both knew this for a blatant lie but neither commented on it beyond a *faux* smile of innocence from Malvina and a derisive snort from her companion.

Malvina glared at him. "What do you want from me now? I have done everything you have ever asked of me. Have you not tortured me enough?"

"Not nearly, my dear lady," he said smoothly. "And now, I have even more reason to require your cooperation."

"Indeed?"

"I want to know what Lord Holt's interest is in you," he replied flatly.

"I have already told you," she said with some asperity. "The blasted man seems to think he is in love with me."

"I have no need to tell you, I think, that he is a detriment to my plans."

Malvina went very still. "What do you plan to do?"

Her companion gave a slow smile. A very malevolent, dangerous smile. "That, my dear, does not concern you."

Those words haunted her for the rest of the day.

Gideon watched Lord Delwyn Deverell leave. His disappointment knew no bounds, but he was unsure with whom he was most disappointed: Malvina for meeting him and concealing her meetings with the man, or the man for stooping low enough to blackmail a lady.

The Duke of Derringer had warned Gideon once. He had said Lord Delwyn was up to something rotten but Gideon had sloughed it off as something minor, like card-sharping. Treason had surely never occurred to him, but he should have known better than to discount a warning from Derringer. The duke never got himself involved in anyone's affairs unless it was of great interest to him. Cheating at cards would surely not rate very high on his scale of importance.

This, however, was of military importance, and Malvina Brackney was neck deep into it. He groaned. His own problems were getting in the way of discovering how to help her. He had to put aside his guilt toward Samantha, his growing feelings for Lady Malvina, and get on with tripping up Deverell.

All of which was much easier said than done. Samantha was a constant ache gnawing at his insides. And now, a friend he thought he'd known well was blackmailing the woman for whom he happened to have some very strong feelings.

Damnation.

Attempting a nonchalance that he was far from feeling, Gideon was once again his usual, lazily charming self. As they sat down for an intimate family dinner, he watched Malvina, noticing the many suspicious glances she sent his way. Her unease was revealed in her green eyes, turmoil and insecurity apparent in every movement of her beautiful body.

"How was your afternoon, my dear?" he asked. His pale brows rose when she choked on her roast beef.

Delicately blotting her mouth with her napkin, she forced a smile while her son stared at her as if she'd lost her mind. "Uneventful. And yours, my lord?"

Gideon frowned. "Uneventful as well, I'm afraid. I fear country life does not suit me. There are too many rats in the grain stores this year and I find such things tedious."

Did he imagine the slight coloring of his betrothed's countenance? Or was he so desperate to see a sign of her guilt that he imagined a reaction where there was none?

Guilt would imply that she felt some remorse for her incautious action in meeting her adversary. It mattered little at this point.

Downing his wine, he asked, "Ride with me in the morning?"

Gideon's hand clenched. Where the devil had that request come from? It was not what he'd intended to say.

Looking startled, Malvina acquiesced.

Annoyed with himself, Gideon shifted the conversation and let Samantha rattle on about her horses for the remainder of the meal.

Malvina awoke to the sounds of her temporary maid, Maddy, entering with chocolate and toast. Yawning, she stretched her arms above her head, a sleepy smile tipping her lips. Some secretive delight filled her, an unknown excitement suffusing her limbs until all she wanted to do was smile.

The shining sun and singing birds could not take credit, surely. She glanced toward the window and remembered. She was to go riding with Lord Holt, her betrothed. The mere thought of spending time in his company was enough to send ripples of delight up and down her spine.

And on that thought came the chilling reminder that she barely knew him. She frowned. Exciting or not, the man was secretive and mysterious. She was still unsure exactly what he wanted with her and her son. He wanted to catch *That Man* but there was something else that had led him to her. It was mere chance that he stumbled upon her during a robbery.

Shaking her head, she set aside her breakfast and rose, smiling as Maddy returned to help her dress. She donned a flattering maroon habit of soft Merino wool with gold frogs in the military style. Her hat was carefully positioned atop her upswept curls.

Satisfied with her appearance, she dismissed the maid. She drew in a deep breath and left the room.

Riding was not Malvina's strong suit, but she was by no means an amateur. Her feeling for horses was mere indifference, not fear. They were necessary for survival and nothing more.

She wisely kept this opinion to herself when in the company of Lady Samantha, whose deep love for her horses was quite apparent. The child actually had an active role in the breeding and training of her precious animals.

Malvina wondered why the countess allowed her daughter to take part in so indelicate an operation.

Gideon waited for her at the front door. She smiled at him without reserve, realizing she would never be able to think of him as *the earl* or *Holt*. His mother called him Holt, but Malvina could see right away that the woman cared more for appearances and "correct behavior" than showing any sort of tenderness toward her children.

Malvina prayed she never felt that way about her own son.

Her betrothed swept her an elegant bow, offering his arm. "You are in looks this fine morning, my dear," he told her gallantly. Leaning in, he added for her ears alone, "Quite delectable, in fact."

She blushed, as he'd intended, the beast.

Ignoring her reaction, she said gaily, "Thank you, my lord."

Moving out into the early morning sun, she asked, "Where do we ride, my lord?" They moved down the steps, approaching two impatiently waiting horses.

"So formal, Malvina," he intoned, tossing her into the saddle of a beautiful chestnut palfrey. Malvina settled herself as comfortably as possible—how comfortable could one actually be in a sidesaddle?—and smiled down at him.

"Where do we ride, Giddy?"

He scowled at her teasing. "I despise that name. I do wish Sammy would cease using it."

He mounted his black hunter, and urged the horse to move. Malvina's animal automatically followed suit. Malvina recognized the animal he rode. It was the same black beast he'd used to rescue her mere weeks ago—a lifetime ago, it seemed. That same black horse who'd traveled with them all the way to Yorkshire, tied behind their carriage. Malvina strongly suspected Samantha wasn't the only one fond of horses.

"Have you perhaps considered that Lady Samantha despises your appellation for her as much as you despise her appellation for you?"

"Sammy?" She could hear the frown in his tone. Gideon swiveled around to look at her face. "Do you suppose so? I hadn't thought."

Malvina urged her horse closer, for the moment oblivious to where they were going. "Sammy is a boy's appellation. Is it not time to start treating her as the young lady she is?"

Gideon's face took on a slightly closed expression, the only indication of his feelings visible in his brown eyes. "Perhaps," he allowed. "I wonder if Sam would agree with you, however."

"Why would she not?"

"For fear that she may then be required to behave as a lady."

Malvina's look of disbelief was almost comical. "I found her to be very ladylike, my lord. In what why could she improve?"

"None," replied Gideon with a touch of bitterness. "I have little doubt, however, that her pastime of horse breeding may cause some to think less kindly of her."

Her brow smoothing out in understanding, Malvina confided, "I did wonder how your mother allowed such an interest in her daughter."

This comment received the opposite reaction that Malvina expected. Lord Holt laughed. Loudly. Enough to startle his companion's deceptively mild horse into rearing up.

Malvina was not prepared for the horse's reaction. The animal reared up and as she came back down, her rider did not.

Well, not immediately anyway.

Showing how very alert he actually was, Gideon threw himself from his own horse and managed to catch Malvina before she struck the ground. She struck *him* hard enough, however, to send them both tumbling into the grass.

Gideon, of course, received the brunt of the impact. He grunted as his back connected with ground that appeared softer than it actually was. Malvina sprawled on top of him, an inelegant heap of woman who struggled to breathe. Whoever would have thought landing on a man could feel as though one smacked a stone?

Face and tone clouded with concern, the man beneath her asked, "Are you hurt?"

She shook her head, more emphatically than necessary, causing an extra bit of dizziness. Pausing, she assured him she was unhurt.

Gideon's eyes roved over her delicate features, searching for signs of injury. He shoved his hands through her red curls, searching her head for bumps, effectively ruining her coiffure and knocking her hat to the ground. Malvina couldn't help but smile at the visible relief on his face when he realized she was quite well.

Her smile disappeared. Lord Holt was suddenly staring into her eyes, his expression deadly serious. Becoming aware of her position—Dear heavens, she was lying on him like a wanton!—Malvina gasped.

Seeking to brace herself, Lady Brackney placed her
hands on the earl's shoulders. Her eyes widened. No
wonder it felt as though she'd struck rock! The muscles of
his upper body were solid stone. Malvina struggled to free
herself, embarrassed that she felt breathless all over again
for a very different reason.

Gideon pinned her to his chest with one arm while
the other hand entangled in her soft hair. He proceeded to
kiss her senseless.

Malvina's bones turned to liquid, her body melting
into his as he plundered her mouth. She no longer cared
that they lay in an open meadow, their mounts chomping
grass a few feet away. All she cared about, in that moment,
was the man beneath her, threatening to send her entire
being up in flames.

It was his horse who recalled them to their
surroundings. He impatiently nudged his master in the
shoulder, nibbled on Gideon's hat, then pawed the ground
right near the man's head. When that was ineffective, the
horse nudged Malvina hard enough to knock her to the
ground.

"Oooo!"

Unfortunately, Gideon's hand was still tangled in her
hair.

"A moment, my dear," he murmured, trying to gently
disengage himself without hurting her further. He smiled at

her when he managed the task, his lips twitching suspiciously as he sat up.

Shoving the horse's nose away from his face, he offered Malvina his hand, helping her sit up as well. Her dark red locks fell all around her face, obscuring her expression. He suspected she was a trifle embarrassed.

When her shoulders started to shake, he was alarmed for her. Was she hurt, after all?

He pulled her hands away from her face. "What is it?" Smoothing the hair from her eyes, he searched for signs of injury again, thinking perhaps he had missed something earlier. Indeed, perhaps she had been hurt by Black. At the thought, he was a little alarmed at the feeling of rage he felt for his horse.

Malvina laughed. "I am quite all right, Gideon, truly. It is merely...it is all so funny!"

He sat back. "Funny, is it?"

"Yes." She spread her arms, encompassing everything around them, from the grass beneath them to the complacent horse standing nearby. "This. Everything. I did everything I was ever instructed to do. From the time I was born, I was ever the dutiful daughter, the faithful wife, the loving mother. I never varied. I never changed. I did what was expected, what was ordered, and what was necessary." She shook her head. "All for naught. No matter what I do, it is not the right thing."

Gideon listened carefully, hearing far more in her diatribe than she intended to reveal. He understood her a little better and was disgusted with what she'd been through, and the fact that he'd put her through a little more.

It was not much different for other women of their station and those raised to enter their station. Women were not taught to think for themselves. Heaven forbid one of them tell her husband or father that she was not pleased with his tyranny!

"You really ought to read Wollstonecraft, my love."

Her wide green eyes reflected her total shock at his words. The works of Mary Wollstonecraft had been forbidden in her father's and her husband's homes. Both men had thought the woman was a meddler, troublemaker, and no better than she should be.

Malvina's mother had done little to counter such beliefs, feeling it was easier to just do as one was told instead of thinking too much about it. One wouldn't want to injure the weak female brain, after all.

Malvina had heard bits and pieces about Mary Wollstonecraft over the years, knew she had had a relationship with a man to whom she was not married. This fact disgusted Malvina enough to avoid anything the woman had ever written.

Gideon's comments on her own seeming innocence although widowed were not far off. She'd only ever known her husband intimately and she firmly believed those intimacies were reserved for marriage.

Until she'd met Gideon, she was sure she'd never stray from that belief. Yet a few moments with his lips against hers was enough to send her good intentions into permanent hiding. What had come over her?

Answering her look of confusion, he told her, "You have always done what you were commanded, Malvina. Look where it has gotten you. Why have you never questioned your course in life?"

"Am I allowed to, then, my lord? Forgive me if I hesitate. The *gentlemen* in my life have never been very forgiving, you see."

Gideon stood and held out his hand. "Your life has changed. Embrace the change and decide for yourself what is right and what is wrong."

10

Everyone sensed a change in Lady Malvina. Upon her return to Moorview Park, she sequestered herself in her room and refused to see or speak to anyone.

Malvina was thinking. She didn't like change but knew the futility of railing against it. When her husband had died, she'd changed nothing. It was far more comfortable to go on as before, as if he were still there, demanding how things should be. It occurred to her, finally, that perhaps that was not the best thing for her son.

When *That Man* had contacted her, fear allowed her to do everything he demanded, assisting his band of cutthroats to lure certain gentlemen of fortune and position into his trap. He'd moved his chosen servants to her home, installed his own men in her stables, and made it clear that she could do nothing without his knowledge. Fear had kept her pinned closely to his side, being an unwilling party to more and more heinous crimes. Always, he threatened not her, but her son. And now, because she wouldn't—or couldn't—think for herself, the death of an innocent young man hung on her conscience.

Then Gideon swooped in and rescued her. She'd likely have gone on doing everything *That Man* asked, right up until he put a bullet through her own head and taken care of Wolf the same way. She'd done nothing in her life for herself, nothing to determine the way she wanted her life to go. While having a child would, naturally, curb any reckless decisions, that wouldn't have prevented a change in scenery. Had she decided after Brackney's death that she would live for herself and her son, she'd have moved the child as far from home as she could afford. She saw now that she should have.

An hour or so after returning from her ride, Malvina heard a knock at her door. She attempted to ignore it but the visitor was persistent. Rising, she flung open the door.

Gideon stood there, his expression deadly serious. He held out a book.

"I apologize for the time it took me to find this." He glanced down at the book he offered, then back at her. "I believe my mother is a little like you. It is easier to do as one is told rather than learn for oneself how one should go on in life."

Malvina reluctantly took his offering. She turned the leatherbound volume over in her hand and opened it. It was Mary Wollstonecraft's *A Vindication of the Rights of Woman*. Glancing back up at her betrothed, she was not as surprised to find him gone as she'd been to find him there at all.

Backing slowly away, Malvina closed the door, amazed. She returned to her seat by the window, set the book on the seat beside her, and stared at it for a long time. Then, she burst into tears.

Gideon left Malvina to her tears and her personal growth. He knew it was easy to tell others to change, but not so easy to tell oneself.

He found his feet taking him to the one room he'd planned to avoid the entirety of his visit; indeed, for the rest of his life. It was empty of human life, an unsurprising circumstance. He moved around the room, drawing back the heavy damask curtains, staring at everything.

The room looked neglected, but not entirely forgotten. Someone cleaned periodically, just enough to keep the worst of the grime at bay without disturbing the contents.

In one corner sat a desk, covered in papers and books, slightly dusty and plainly ignored. No one had bothered to return the books to the library or neatly stack the papers.

Gideon turned, one hand clenched. In the middle of the room was a long table. On it sat bottles and beakers, more papers, quills and ink, and another book, open to a certain page. On one end was a microscope, the most advanced and expensive available nine years ago.

His parents had ordered this room to be left alone. It was to be a shrine to Samantha's beauty, a constant reminder of Gideon's wrongs.

It wasn't the room or even the home where it had happened. But this had been his sanctuary, science his escape. So he understood their actions.

They didn't seem to realize he was fully capable of punishing himself and with far greater severity than they could have ever devised.

He sighed. Moving to the center table, he stared down at its contents, wondering just what he'd been thinking all those years ago.

He absently fingered a brown bottle, long since empty. The old earl had had some presence of mind, then. He'd seen fit to rid the premises of the chemicals his son had loved so well.

It was for the best, he thought now, gazing around. This room had never produced results and Gideon had been wasting his time playing with such dangerous things.

His hand trembled.

The small bottle he still clutched slipped to the floor, smashing into a million pieces. He stared down at it, unaware of how it had happened.

Samantha was the reason Gideon's life had turned out other than he had originally planned. After disfiguring her so severely, he lost the *joie de vivre* he'd previously enjoyed. It was all he could do to avoid slipping into a melancholy so deep he couldn't climb out.

It was why he became insouciant. And offered his services to the Home Office, tracking down traitors and spies. It was a thankless job, dangerous and often nauseating. What better way to redeem oneself than to hunt down those who willingly hurt others? If one happened to die in the process...

Another bottle joined the first. Blue shards mingled with brown in shafts of early afternoon sun.

His work there had led him to a man who'd been smuggling secrets for years while Bonaparte roamed the world, seeking to conquer the whole. Clues had pointed to Sir Richard Brackney, baronet. He was not the ringleader, however. There was someone above him, a mystery man who moved his people around like pawns on a chess board.

The man's identity was no longer a mystery. It was Gideon's own childhood friend, Lord Delwyn Deverell.

Another bottle smashed, this one several feet from the others.

Since peace with France had been established, Deverell's past activities must have had everything to do with greed and little to do with loyalty to Bonaparte's cause. It had to be the reason he was staging holdups. Gideon could only assume Deverell's ability to use Malvina was blackmail.

With an angry swipe, Gideon cleared the table of the rest of the bottles. He barely heard the crash as they smashed all around the room.

That meant Brackney was guilty. Even after his death, the crown would still want to hold Brackney accountable for his treason. His title and properties would be seized, his family ostracized, hounded from Society.

Gideon's mother would truly go into a decline if he married Lady Brackney.

Books and papers flew, adding to the worsening destruction of Gideon's once-precious room.

He leaned against the table, hands fisted tightly, trying to dam up the rage, trying to convince himself that visible emotion was a weakness. It was never productive to allow the feelings release.

There was one glaring incongruity in Deverell's actions that made Gideon distinctly nervous. Why did the man visit Malvina in person? Was he that confident he would not be caught?

Or was there actually someone pulling his strings as he pulled Malvina's?

Releasing a cry of frustrated rage, the noble Earl of Holt lifted the heavy table and threw it across the room. The microscope, beakers, and sundry other items flew, smashed, crashed, and banged all around him.

It did not relieve the helpless frustration that consumed him.

"Very mature, Giddy."

He had not heard the door open. He turned to find Samantha staring at him, her brown eyes filled with concern.

He sighed, pinching the bridge of his nose. "You should not be here."

"Nor should you." She walked toward him, her slippered feet moving silently around the debris. She stopped before him, searching his features for clues as to his behavior. "What has come over you?"

He shrugged, slipping back into his comfortable, insouciant façade.

Lady Samantha struck him on the chest. "Don't you dare become the lifeless care-for-nothing, Giddy! I hate that."

She stepped back, looking very much as if she'd like to hit him again. She successfully employed ladylike restraint but stepped back again to avoid the temptation.

"Why are you here?" he asked.

"I come here every day."

Astonishment exploded in his chest. "Why the *devil* would you do that?"

She shrugged. "To remember you." Gazing around at the destruction he'd so effortlessly wrought, she added, "Today, however, it is not the same."

He would not cry. How completely stupid to feel hurt, sorrow, or sadness that she would want to constantly remind herself that her only brother had permanently harmed her.

"Is not your mirror sufficient to remind you ?"

She met his gaze, her brow furrowed in confusion. Staring into his ever-revealing eyes, she realized what he implied.

"I do not come here to wallow in misery and hate, Giddy," she told him gently. "I come here to remember *you*. I miss you. I miss the old you, the one who was up to every rig and row. The one who teased me and laughed at me and told me when I vexed you. The one who pretended I was an irritating younger sister but never failed to include me."

She squeezed his arm. "I never hated you, Giddy." She gestured to her face, making him wince at the severity of her scars. "Not for this. I hated you for changing and for leaving. I hated you for treating me as though I was different. I hated you for revealing you were just like everyone else, believing appearances were more important than what was inside. I needed you, Giddy, to make me laugh, when the pain was so bad all I could do was cry."

She searched his features for he knew not what, the intensity of her gaze sending a twinge of alarm through him. Her next words stunned him unlike any others.

"I needed you to tell me I was to blame."

Gideon stared helplessly at her, watching the tears well up in her huge eyes and trickle down her cheeks. Her face turned red and splotchy, causing the scars to stand out, grotesquely ugly against the purity of the girl they marked. She clutched at his sleeve, begging him to understand the ways she felt he'd failed her.

A single tear managed to escape before he could stop it. Damming the wellspring, he shook her off. He was not ready to give up any of the blame in the situation.

Samantha pressed her rejected hand to her mouth, trying to hold back the sobs that threatened to tear her in two.

"I am doing quite well, today," the calm, emotionless Lord Holt murmured. "I have managed to cause grief to the two women I care about most." He snapped a bow. "Permit me to leave you so I may visit Mother and see what I may do to her."

Samantha watched him leave. When the door closed, she sank to the floor in an elegant heap, her sobs released from deep within.

The next day, Malvina had read the book loaned to her and found it to be very enlightening. While she couldn't care for Mary Wollstonecraft herself or condone many of her personal choices, Malvina was wise enough to see the logic in the woman's teachings and understand the frustration she must have felt at her lot in life.

It made sense to Malvina that women were as capable as men of learning, thought, and logic. It also made sense that men would feel threatened by a woman learning to think for herself.

What didn't make sense was her betrothed encouraging her to do just that.

Further confused by the enigma that was Lord Holt, Malvina entered the breakfast room earlier than was her wont. It was surprisingly empty, even of servants. Curious, she turned around and went in search of another human.

When the house yielded no results, she walked through the front door. A silent scream rose up to choke her at the sight that met her eyes.

Gideon was trying to kill her baby!

The two men were stripped to shirtsleeves and stockinged feet, moving back and forth in a dance of death, silver foils flashing in the late morning sunlight.

Malvina strode forward, intent on ending the contretemps, little heeding the flash of metal as their weapons met time and again.

Someone reached out and stopped her before she'd made it three steps. Shockingly, it was Keeley, the butler. She was about to reprimand the man for laying hands on her person when she became aware that Lady Samantha had approached and stood watching at her side.

"Could you not have stopped him, my lady. He is your brother."

The sound that issued from Lady Samantha's delicate throat closely resembled a snort. "He is not my brother, Lady Malvina. I have no idea who that man is. Can you not stop him? He is your betrothed. Come to that, the other is your son."

Throwing a glare at the importuning butler, she muttered, "I am not to be allowed to interfere, I think."

In that moment, Wolf released a snarl and lunged at the earl. Malvina held her breath, unsure for whom she was most afraid. A second later, her son was disarmed, his foil flying through the air to stick in the ground at her feet. She was momentarily startled, realizing that had she been standing even one foot closer, she'd have been skewered.

Her heart beating in her throat, she glanced up to see Gideon holding his sword at her son's neck. Maternal instinct took over. She determinedly shook off the butler's restraining hand, snatched up the foil at her feet, and marched over to the combatants.

Malvina didn't think. She snapped the foil up and pressed it beneath Lord Holt's chin. "Release him!"

Brows quirking slightly at her, Gideon obeyed. His foil fell away from Wolf's throat while Malvina's dipped slightly. Suddenly, she found herself disarmed.

It was unclear to her how it had happened. One second, she was holding the earl at bay, heart hammering in her throat, and the next, her weapon was gone and she was being marched into the manor with a very angry betrothed at her side.

He paused only long enough to retrieve his boots and outer garments

Leaning close, he murmured lowly, "When I said you need to think for yourself, I did not mean to imply you should make stupid, thoughtless decisions that put your life in danger."

"Stupid, thoughtless...! How dare you, sir! You tried to kill my baby!"

Shoving her through the first door he came to, Gideon's reply was succinct. "He is not a baby, Malvina. He's a man now and so damned confused about it that he has no idea how to go on."

His words silenced her for a mere second. "How is assaulting him supposed to solve that?"

"I was not assaulting him," her companion sighed. He threw his outer garments aside and sat down to pull on his boots. "He came at me with murder in his eyes and I gave him the chance, merely."

She was visibly horrified. "You gave him the chance? Are you mad?"

He looked up. "I knew he could not win, Malvina."

"You *were* trying to hurt him!"

Standing, he watched her hands clench. He caught her before she managed to use them on him. Drawing her closer, he said, "I was not going to hurt him. Only teach him a lesson."

"What lesson is that? Violence solves all arguments?"

"That he is not invincible and should not go through life with the mistaken belief that he is."

Silenced, Malvina stopped struggling. She was duly released and used the opportunity to move away from Lord Holt. "I do not care for your methods," she told him calmly.

"I did not expect that you would," he informed her. "Hence, the reason you were not informed."

She stared at him, her green eyes shimmering suspiciously. "Is this the way it will be, my lord? Will I have no say in my own son?"

Closing the distance between them, Gideon grasped her upper arms. "I am not usurping your position as the boy's parent. I am trying to help guide him in a way that you cannot."

Her chin rose a notch. "Why can I not? I am just as intelligent as you."

He laughed, the wretch. Placing gentle fingers on her cheek, his other hand slid over her back. "No one is debating that, love. But you are not a man and what that boy needs is a father."

Her anger deflated. "What am I to do with him?"

"Dare I suggest you trust me?"

He drew her closer. She stared up at him, not sure how to answer him. The effect his nearness was having on her breathing did not help matters.

Gideon's hands found their way into her hair, tipping her face up to his. Mesmerized, she didn't pull away. She moved her hands to his waist and pulled him closer and closed her eyes.

"You have trusted every man you've ever met. Why do you not trust me?"

Her eyes snapped open. Blinking slowly, she replied, "You are not what you seem. You hold yourself and your thoughts away, revealing only what you want known."

She found herself released and standing alone by the time she finished her words. Her emotions jolted severely when he simply looked at her with his typical sleepy expression, the very expression he employed to hide something.

"When involved with a woman like you, a man must protect himself."

"And you want to marry me."

Malvina was surprised at the confidence in her tone. She finally believed he wanted to marry her. Suspicion whispered in her ear, however, a sneaking belief that whoever had ordered him to investigate her had not told him to marry her.

She was unpleasantly surprised when her betrothed again took her arms with no gentleness. "Oh, I have my reasons for wanting to marry you, Lady Malvina Brackney. It does not mean I will ever trust you. How can I? You send young men to their deaths for...what? Money?"

Hard green eyes snapping in anger, she told him, "Of course. What other reason is there for criminal behavior?" She wrenched her arms free and slammed both hands into his chest. He stumbled back, taken by surprise. With what sounded suspiciously like a growl, she added, "Of course there is no money involved, Lord Holt. It only ever was blackmail."

He smiled. "Why?"

She hesitated, considering a lie. Realizing he would see right through it, she opted for silence instead.

His smile turned grim. "I see. Why are *you* marrying *me*?"

Malvina moved to a chair near the window and sat. She gave him an unreadable look. "You possess what every woman desires, my lord earl. Title, fortune, good looks. A woman can be sure she will never starve, she will have all the envy of her peers, and may be reasonably attracted to the man who claims possession of her body. Why would I not marry you?"

He seemed stunned. As though her claim was not something he'd ever considered before. "How very logical," he murmured finally, "for a woman in your position. Let us hope you do not find your marital duties too unpleasant."

"Logical?" she shot back, ignoring the rest of his comment. "It is not logical. It is mercenary and cruel. Do you not mind being considered a mere object to be used?"

"My, my. You are an innocent, are you not? One would never think it to consider your age."

Wounded and unwilling to show it, she said, "Quite. One wonders why you want such an old woman in your bed."

"Perhaps I am a bit like Prinny. I find myself attracted to women who could be my mother."

It was perhaps fortunate that the door slammed open before she had a chance to reply to *that* vexing remark.

Her son marched in, violence radiating from every line. She repressed a shiver at the fierce image he presented, his dark red hair falling about his face and giving him a half-crazed look. Was his anger directed at her, or Lord Holt?

Glaring at the earl, Wolf snarled, "What have you done to her?"

Gideon's brows quirked upward. "I have done nothing. I was preparing to ravish her but you have rudely interrupted."

Malvina's eyes grew impossibly huge. She placed herself between her son and betrothed when she realized the former was about to attack the latter.

"He is jesting, Wolf," she tried to reassure her child. It did not help that Gideon took advantage of her position by drawing her back against him. "He is in an impossible mood." A well-placed elbow in the ribs made the man step back. "I was about to do him an injury, in all honesty."

She magnanimously chose to ignore the disbelieving snort from the man behind her.

Approaching her only child, she asked, "Are you injured?"

"Injured?"

"From the fight outside." She looked him over, searching for signs of blood and bruising. She missed the embarrassed look on her son's face.

Gideon saw it. "My dear, perhaps you can give me a moment to discuss this matter with Wolf. It is, unfortunately, a matter between gentlemen."

A little affronted, Malvina nevertheless agreed. She left the room in a bit of a huff.

Gideon and Wolf eyed each other with distrust and unease. The elder had little experience with young men and the younger had little trust for adults in general.

"I realize you don't want to replace your father," Gideon began.

"Not for the reason you think."

The earl stared. "What was your father involved in?"

"Why should I tell you? I don't think you are exactly who you say you are. Sure, you're an earl, but I want to know why you are after my family."

New respect for young Sir Beowulf filled Gideon's mind. He studied the boy's defensive stance—crossed arms, narrowed eyes, tensed shoulders—and knew he would lie to protect his mother even if it meant angering the man who questioned him.

"Be at ease, Wolf," the earl told him. He gestured for the boy to sit, lowering himself into another chair. "I was not sent to destroy you. My superiors merely want answers."

"Who are they?" The young baronet finally sat, openly surprised that his companion admitted he was at the beck and call of someone else.

Gideon debated what to reveal and decided to trust the boy to an extent. He needed the boy's cooperation if he were to discover a way to prove Deverell's guilt, and determine whether or not there was any truth to the suspicion of Sir Richard Brackney's treasonous activities.

His observations to date did not lean heavily in favor of the late baronet.

"I work for the Home Office," he said, deciding there was little harm in the boy knowing that much.

A glimmer of what appeared to be genuine interest lit Wolf's dark blue eyes. "Ferreting out spies and the like?"

"Among other things," was Gideon's careful reply.

"That sounds dashed exciting. Have you ever been shot?"

"No. I hope never to be shot."

"Are you here to catch the cur blackmailing my mother?"

Gideon felt a partial truth answered best. "Yes."

The large young man visibly relaxed, slumping a little in his chair. "So your engagement is merely a ruse. Dashed relief, that."

Ignoring the pinprick he felt, Gideon swiftly disabused his companion of such a belief. "Why should you think it merely a ruse?"

Wolf's forehead wrinkled, a hank of long dark red hair falling into his eyes. He impatiently shoved it back. "You are younger than her. You cannot possibly want to marry an older woman."

Gideon's lips quirked ever so slightly. "Why not?" He leaned back and watched carefully as the boy tried to understand how a man could possibly find Lady Malvina Brackney attractive.

Wolf opened his mouth several times before finally saying, "She's old."

"You do realize I am only four years her junior?"

"That's all? You appear much younger than you are."

"Thank you for that tactless observation. I am forever underestimated for my appearance."

His face clearing considerably, Sir Beowulf Brackney confided, "As am I."

"Indeed," the earl murmured with interest. "Then perhaps you will do me the honor of not referring to my age or appearance with such regularity."

Wolf had the grace to flush. "Sorry."

"Do you return home for holidays?"

A little startled by the turn of the conversation, Wolf hesitated. "Not always. Father liked me to come home but I was inclined to visit Claremont."

"Claremont?"

"Lord Preston's heir. Deveraux, Earl of Claremont. I stay with his family when I can. Father didn't always allow it but Mama could usually persuade him."

How curious. "Your mother encouraged the connection?"

"Of course. Father did, as well, but Mama did seem to prefer me to stay with Claremont instead of coming home." He paused, his face creasing in thought. "In fact, there were times when Mama was quite adamant that I not come home. I didn't think much of it at the time."

"Before or after your father's death?"

"Both." He met Gideon's eyes. "Could she have been trying to keep the robberies from me?"

"Most probably. Many mothers would not want their children involved in their problems. Considering your temper, Malvina was probably terrified you'd do something brash and get yourself killed."

The hotheaded baronet shot to his feet. "I would never...!"

"Never...what?" the earl interrupted. He gazed up at his soon-to-be stepson, silently amused at the young man's defensive response. "You would never charge in, hell for leather, intent on bodily injury?"

Wolf glared, an incongruous expression when his face was slowly turning red in embarrassment. He opened his mouth but nothing emerged. Instead, he turned and stormed from the room.

Given much to ponder, the earl didn't follow for several minutes. When he reached the door, he was prevented by the entrance of his mother, an occurrence that surprised a reaction from him.

"Mother, what the devil?"

She frowned at her only son. "Must you use such coarse language, Holt? I blame *That Woman's* influence."

Her use of *'That Woman'* reminded him so much of Malvina that he actually laughed. Apologizing quickly, he added, "My betrothed's influence has little to do with my language, Mother."

She sniffed, moving further into the room. Sinking gracefully into the chair just vacated by her son, she made use of her ever-present *sal volatile* and murmured plaintively, "She is upsetting the household, Holt. You must curb her inclination to meddle."

"How can she have been meddling? She has only been from my side for an hour."

"She is with Samantha, asking all sorts of improper questions about those horses and weapons and any number of vulgar things. I do not want someone of her ilk influencing my daughter."

Gideon's face took on a closed expression, his lids drooping to conceal his eyes. After learning how she had protected her son from the ugliness she couldn't control, he knew Lady Malvina Brackney would never harm Samantha.

"You go too far, Mother," he warned softly. "Lady Malvina may not have been born in the upper echelons of

Society but she is a lady. She is also a mother and would never do anything to harm Samantha."

Lady Holt's eyes snapped dangerously. "She harms her by bringing that malefactor into my home," she uttered darkly, the loathing in her voice a surprise to the son who'd mostly known her as a discontented lover of tonics and powders. "She harms her by encouraging her in unladylike pursuits. She is determined to finish what you started eight years ago."

Bowing, the Earl of Holt said, "Good day, Mother. We will depart for London in a few days time."

Lady Malvina was of two minds about going to church. She did not know what rumors flew around the neighboring estates and she had no desire to know. It was not improper for her to visit her betrothed's family, but she was the daughter of a London merchant. Marrying a baronet could not change that fact in some narrow minds. Trapping an eligible earl would endear her to no one.

Maddy informed her mistress upon entering her chamber that the master was desirous of attending services that morning and would her ladyship join him?

Hardly able to decline, her ladyship agreed.

The family party, Lord Holt, Lady Malvina, Sir Beowulf and Lady Samantha, arrived at the quaint little Norman church in time to be seated. They arrived late enough to avoid having to accept toadying compliments from those who would further their position in Society.

Gideon's eyes scanned the assemblage as they moved to the family pew in the front of the church. Dr. Phelps, the reverend whose living belonged to the earldom of Holt, nodded but didn't smile. He was notoriously sour-faced.

In a pew near the back sat a man who did not belong. He smiled in a friendly fashion at Lord Holt, tipped his hat to Lady Malvina and Lady Samantha, and gave Wolf an appraising glance.

Malvina faltered in her trek to the front. She stumbled against Gideon, who steadied her with a hand on her elbow and guided her the rest of the way.

"Are you well?" he asked as he seated her.

She smiled, nodding her head. "Indeed. I merely trod on my hem."

Gideon accepted her excuse. He knew full well what had her so skittish. Deverell sat in the back of the Church, bold as brass. Gideon could say nothing to indicate he knew of the man's connection to Malvina. He had to behave as though he was actually glad to see his old school chum.

He clenched his jaw and nodded to Dr. Phelps. The old curmudgeon's stentorian voice boomed out, causing the Brackneys to jump. The reverend's voice was something else and quite startling to someone unaccustomed to it.

As the good reverend boomed out his sermon on the wages of sin, Malvina fretted about that very thing. The stranger at the back of the church was *That Man* and she had little doubt he was there for her.

The sermon ended rather abruptly when Lord Holt gave the reverend an exasperated look. He dismissed the congregation and scowled at the earl. Gideon smiled lazily back.

Being very careful to behave as Deverell would expect, Gideon waited to be approached. He sensed the tension in his betrothed and resisted the urge to reveal his knowledge of her tormentor's identity.

The only thing that kept Gideon from truly donning his relaxed, lazy persona was the fact that Deverell was not attempting to hide. What was he involved in that gave him such a feeling of security?

There was one possibility that gave Gideon a chill down his spine. If Deverell planned to kill Malvina, there was no need to conceal himself. He certainly had her terrified enough to keep his connection with her a secret. If Deverell suspected that Gideon was trying to help her, however...

Lord Holt was wise enough to realize that Deverell did, in fact, suspect his involvement with the widow. Gideon would have to tread carefully.

Greeting each other amiably, the gentlemen talked of trivialities for a moment. Then, turning to his companions, Gideon performed the introductions.

"Lord Delwyn Deverell, my betrothed, Lady Malvina and her son, Sir Beowulf Brackney. You remember my sister, Lady Samantha."

"Indeed," Deverell murmured, favoring Lady Samantha with a charming smile. She smiled back but Gideon could tell she wasn't the least impressed with the man.

Deverell shook Wolf's hand and turned to Lady Malvina. Donning his most charming manner, he kissed the air above her hand. "Holt is a most fortunate man, my lady."

Malvina barely suppressed the shudder that threatened at his touch. Smiling back, she murmured the appropriate response and drew her hand back. Her eyes widened when she realized he had transferred a twist of paper into her palm.

Wanting nothing more than to toss it into his smug face, she instead slipped it into her reticule. She could not be sure if Gideon saw; he missed little.

After returning to the Moorview Park, Malvina managed to find a moment alone when she changed for luncheon. Opening the little spill of paper, she read the few words, frowning.

*Old folly. Half past one.*

Glancing at her mantel clock, she realized it only lacked fifteen minutes to the designated time. Not bothering to ring for Maddy, she scrambled into a sturdy walking dress. Tying on her bonnet, she left her room, being careful to avoid everyone. She didn't like to lie and felt avoiding the necessity was the best plan.

She followed a well-worn path from the house to the edge of the estate. The old folly stood to the north, near a pond. The first Earl of Holt had it built shortly before follies became all the rage. Some estate owners had even hired a man or instructed a servant to play the part of a hermit to enhance the ambiance of the setting.

Malvina approached the small tower, wondering why the current earl did not have it torn down. It was more of an eyesore than it was romantic. Checking the watch fob pinned to her bosom, she realized she was nearly five minutes late.

What revenge would Lord Delwyn Deverell take if he thought she had not appeared?

She nearly jumped from her skin when the man in question appeared from behind a large rock. How appropriate it was for him to lurk near rocks. Very snakelike.

"Lord Delwyn, is it? What a relief it is to be able to put a name with the face," she said, trying—and failing—to keep the biting sarcasm from her voice.

"There is no need for you not to know," he replied. "How are you adjusting to your engagement?"

"I will not discuss any aspect of my personal life with you, sir. Say what you have come to say and begone."

He smiled. "Ah. Straight to the point. A woman after my own heart."

His comment made her slightly sick but Malvina refused to be drawn.

"There is a certain document, I am given to understand, that resides within the home of Lord Holt. Perhaps you would be so good as to retrieve it for me."

"What kind of document?"

"A simple list, nothing more. Names and dates, amounts of money. Nothing important."

"Then why do you want it?"

"My reasons need not concern you. Only be aware that your precious earl will bear the brunt of my anger if you do not cooperate."

She felt suddenly faint. She was quite sure her face dramatically paled. "Excuse me?"

"I am upping the ante, my dear lady. Your cooperation will safeguard Lord Holt. My superiors do not care for his interference and would like to see him"—he paused —"removed. I may be able to convince them otherwise."

"He is your friend. How can you do this to him?"

"He is a childhood acquaintance, nothing more. Besides, there are more important matters to consider than mere friendship."

Malvina could only nod her assent to his demands, any words she might have spoken strangling on her tongue. She glanced away, fighting the urge to clear the nonexistent blockage from her throat.

Finally, she returned her eyes to her companion, biting back the words she really wanted to say, asking instead, "How will I know the correct document?"

"I'll make this easy for you," her companion said with false concern. "Bring me every document matching my description."

Malvina nodded and moved away. "Will you then return my husband's journal?"

Lord Delwyn studied her, his eyes sharply aware of every nuance of her expression. "The chances are greater, to be sure."

Unsatisfied but able to do little about it, Malvina left him. She didn't look back.

13

The logical place to look was the earl's study. Good fortune—if one could call it that—smiled on her the following day.

Gideon had just that morning left for London, informing them all that his business was urgent and he must travel alone, on horseback. They waved him off and Malvina breathed a sigh, relieved. It was one less thing for her to fret over, one less person to catch her at her despicable task.

She left her chamber quickly, eager to be done with the whole sorry business. After a cursory knock on the study door, she entered.

The study was typically masculine. Sturdy furniture, dark colors, shelves of books, stacks of documents and no hint of femininity anywhere to be found.

Malvina groaned. The large desk was positively covered in papers. It would take her several hours to sift through them.

She strode forward, clenching her fists in an abstracted manner. Who would have thought Gideon would be so very untidy? Although, reflecting on what she knew of the man, Malvina realized that was exactly in keeping with his lazy personality.

She picked up the first stack. A quick look-through revealed it to be nothing more than shopkeeper bills. Placing them back where she found them, she retrieved another stack...

An hour later, she'd gone over every pile on the desk and found exactly nothing matching the description given to her by *That Man*...that is, Lord Delwyn.

Her gaze swept the room. More documents were stuffed haphazardly onto shelves. With a sinking feeling, she looked down. Opening the first drawer in the desk, she found even more. Indeed, Gideon needed a keeper.

Selecting a stack of papers at random, she continued her search. She had just replaced a stack on the bookshelf when the door opened. Her heart thundering, Malvina turned.

Lady Samantha. She inwardly cursed. The mother in her cringed at the thought of Lady Samantha having any inkling of the situation.

"Lady Malvina?"

Forcing a smile to her stiff lips, Malvina said, "Lady Samantha. Were you looking for me?"

"Indeed not. Mother asked me to fetch something for her, an account book." She paused, studying the shelf behind Malvina. Eyes flipping to the woman instead, Samantha asked, "What are you doing in here?"

"Looking for a book," Malvina promptly lied.

"In the study? You'd do better to look in the library. There is nothing in here except boring books on farming methods and such."

"Of course. How silly of me." Moving to leave, she paused next to the girl. "Please do not tell your brother. Such an embarrassment."

After hesitating a mere moment, the young lady agreed. She fetched the account book her mother had sent her for and followed Malvina out.

"Why did Lady Holt not send a servant for the book?" Malvina asked curiously, while wondering why Gideon's mother was interested in the accounts at all. She did not seem like the type of mistress to worry overmuch about it, not while there were new and more interesting illnesses to...contract.

"She did. Charles returned to say that there was someone in the study and he did not want to disturb the occupant."

Casting a sharp glance the girl's way, Malvina was surprised to note the very blandness of her expression. "Your mother allowed this? Is it not odd for a servant to return empty-handed? Do the servants behave so when your brother is in residence?"

Samantha shrugged. "Mother is not so tolerant but it is the way Giddy is. He is forever allowing things to happen that he probably should not."

There was a tone in the younger woman's voice that Malvina could only describe as bitterness. When Lady Samantha absently touched her scarred face, things became somewhat clearer to Malvina.

Placing a gentle hand on her companion's arm, she asked, "What happened to you?"

Samantha stopped, her once pretty features smoothing as much as possible. "A mishap. Nothing more."

"How does it concern Gideon?"

"He was there."

Her response was eloquently unresponsive. "Why do you speak of your brother with such bitterness when it is obvious to the veriest lackwit how much you adore him?"

"Lady Malvina, I do not want to seem rude, but how is that any concern of yours?"

"Your brother is my concern, Lady Samantha. Your bitterness hurts him and his pain is very much my concern."

Samantha's brows rose in surprise. Malvina wondered if she herself was wearing a similar expression. She'd only spoken the truth. It was interesting that she had not known it was the truth until she'd said it aloud.

"If you were so concerned for my brother, you would not have been prying through his things."

Samantha continued her trek, leaving Malvina to stare blindly after her. The watery film over her eyes would not allow her to see clearly.

Gideon returned two days later.

Malvina sat restlessly through dinner. She picked at her food, drank too much wine, and muttered monosyllables to anyone who addressed her directly.

"Is anything distressing you?"

She jumped at Gideon's question, guilt turning her face pink. Forcing a smile to lips that wanted to tremble, she said, "No, indeed. I am merely tired."

He raised disbelieving brows at her excuse but allowed it to stand uncontested.

"Perhaps, then, you would not mind answering my question."

"What question, my lord?"

"How did you find the folly? Was it as romantic as ladies seem to believe such things are?"

Startled by the subject of his inquiry, it was a moment before she answered. "I have never thought there was anything remotely romantic about dangerous ruins. Even man-made ruins."

"Perhaps if a lady were there to meet a gentleman friend. Would that lend a modicum of romance to the setting?"

She couldn't help it. She searched his face, looking for any indication that he knew of her meeting with Lord Delwyn Deverell. His expression was the same lazy, nonthreatening look he'd worn almost every moment since she'd met him. His eyelids drooped over his eyes, concealing his thoughts from her.

He idly swirled the red wine in his glass, watching her rather than the liquid. She saw his fingers spasm on the stem. It was this last that convinced her that he knew.

She sighed.

Gideon glanced at the others present, noticing they were silently eating, trying not to listen. Except Wolf, who craned his neck in an effort to hear every word.

The earl sent a meaningful glance to his mother. The lady rose—forcing the gentlemen to rise as well—and indicated that she was ready to retire to her chamber, as she was feeling quite ill of a sudden. It was broadly hinted that the other ladies retire as well.

Malvina rose to her feet, feeling relieved to escape. She bit back another sigh when Gideon took her hand, tugging her back down into her seat. He released her almost immediately.

"Perhaps it is well for you to retire as well, Sir Beowulf," Gideon added.

To his credit, the young man hesitated. Lady Samantha urged him to obey, whispering something that subtly eased his tension. Everyone filed out, wishing goodnight to the earl and his betrothed.

The earl lowered himself back down to his chair and gestured to the butler. Snapping a smart bow, the butler herded his minions from the room.

A full minute of silence passed before the earl broke it with a question. "What is going on?"

"Going on?"

"You are in the habit of clandestine rendezvous with men you've only just met?"

"Of course not!" she denied hotly. "Are you in the habit of spying on your betrothed's activities?"

"I am in the habit of spying, madam," was his succinct reply. He refilled his wine glass and held the bottle out to his companion. She considered declining the offer but held out her glass instead. "As for spying on my betrothed, you are the first I've ever had and no, it is not what I would typically do. However, under the circumstances..."

"Under the circumstances?" she asked dangerously, her own feelings of guilt rendering a sharpness to her tone that she actually had not intended.

Gideon gave her a disbelieving, slightly contemptuous look. "Please do not play the innocent, Lady Malvina. You are well aware of the reasons I do not trust you. Is it any wonder I am upset to find you have been meeting a gentleman without my knowledge, on my own estate?"

As she opened her mouth to reply, she realized something. There was a certain timbre in his voice that was something she'd never heard before.

At least, not from Gideon.

Her husband had often had just that almost petulant tone in his voice, bordering on anger. It was a familiar sound and, somehow, helped her regain her footing.

"It is not what you suspect, Gideon," she said softly. She reached out to take his hand. He hesitated a moment before clasping hers in turn. "I happened upon Lord Delwyn quite by chance. I was out walking and he was near the folly. I assumed, since you and he are old friends, that he was allowed to wander the grounds. We discussed the weather, nothing more."

His expression hardened for just a moment before smoothing back out. Malvina's breath caught. Did he suspect his friend and *That Man* were one and the same? She couldn't let him know.

Visibly relaxing, Lord Holt smiled. "It is late, my dear. Perhaps you should retire. I shall see you in the morning."

Inwardly miserable at her lies, Malvina wanted to say something, wanted nothing more than to tell him what truly happened. Not able to find the words, she rose.

"Goodnight, Gideon." When he didn't move to follow her out, she turned back. "Do you not retire, as well?"

He tossed back the remainder of his wine. "No, indeed. I believe I shall go out." He grinned at her. "I am not yet tired."

# 14

It was the answer to a prayer.

After her run-in with Lady Samantha, that young lady had been far too watchful of Malvina's activities. Erring on the side of caution, Malvina had postponed her search for the document, hoping for another chance soon. Having exhausted the possibility of the paper residing in the study, Malvina decided to put Gideon's absence to good use. She would search his chamber.

She allowed Maddy to help her into her nightclothes and brush out her long, dark red hair, the soothing strokes having no effect on the nervous energy coursing her veins. She settled in her bed, pretending to read as the maid finished her evening duties.

"You may have the rest of the evening, Maddy," she told her. "It is not too late. I'm sure you can find some enjoyable way to occupy yourself."

Bobbing a curtsy, the maid murmured her thanks. Malvina watched her leave with bated breath. The maid had let slip that Lord Holt's valet had also been given the evening to himself and would be in the butler's sitting room, gambling for farthings.

Allowing several tense minutes to pass, she finally left her chamber and made her way to her betrothed's apartment. Entering, she wandered around, trying to deduce the best place to hide something of critical importance. Perhaps close at hand?

She moved to the nightstand. It was quick work to determine the stand contained nothing more than an old, worn Bible.

A Bible?

Nonplussed at such an odd discovery—she hadn't thought of the earl as a very religious individual—Malvina moved on.

The small writing desk also yielded nothing. She slowly spun, searching with her eyes for anything else that could hide what she sought. Unfortunately, a document could be hidden almost anywhere.

With a long-suffering sigh, she entered his dressing room. The places to look seemed endless. There were three armoires and a dressing table. Drawers and cupboards abounded. How many clothes did a gentleman need?

Squaring her shoulders, she waded in, determined to have this nightmare over.

It was while she was sifting through some papers she found stuffed in a jewel case—the man had more jewels than she'd ever seen in her life!—that she stopped breathing. Pushing her encroaching hair away from her face, she studied the document she held.

It was exactly as *he* had described it. Names, amounts of money, dates. What she found strange was the fact that the dates coincided with the Peninsular Campaign that ended with the defeat of Napoleon nearly five years ago.

More astonishing still was the name of Lord Delwyn Deverell near the middle of the list.

Heart plummeting, her voice whispered across the empty room. "He knew. All along, he knew."

"Not exactly."

She spun, the incriminating document clutched to her chest. "Gideon!"

His slow smile was unexpected. "As I was saying, I didn't exactly know. I but suspected. I have possessed that document for a short time, you see. I'd not had time to more than glance at it."

He moved into the room and gestured to the chair by the dressing table. When she didn't move, he offered, "We can adjourn to the bedroom, but I am not sure how much talking will get done."

She sat.

Grimly amused at her ready capitulation in the face of implied seduction, Gideon moved forward and reached out to take the document from her. She resisted with such a look of panic that he withdrew, curious.

"What threat did he use, Malvina?"

She firmly clamped her lips shut. Amusement at her stubbornness threatened to tip his lips but the gravity of her situation prevented it.

"We can do this the easy way, or the hard way. Your choice."

Her gaze dropped to her lap. She refused to be drawn.

Releasing a sigh, he crouched at her feet. She clutched the paper tighter, creasing it, wadding it into a ball.

"If my superiors discover you know anything about this, you will disappear, Malvina. It will be quite the mystery. One that will never be solved because they do not wish it to be. I do not want to see that happen." With a finger beneath her chin, he forced her to look at him. "I do not want that to happen."

Her gaze was haunted. He hated what she had been through; he hated that he would inevitably put her through yet more. But those men had to be captured. They had led many men to their deaths, needlessly. If one unfortunate widow was caught in the crossfire, it would be overlooked, hushed up.

The idea pained Gideon in a way he did not want to examine. All along, he had told her he would indeed marry her. All along, he had come to terms with the possibility. If it came to that, he would have made a life with her, unable to condone the death of a woman in the name of war.

It had not been in his plans to fall in love with her.

He didn't trust her. She kept dangerous secrets. Her secrets had led to an innocent death, as well. The Home Office might actually view her demise as justice for her wrongs.

Gideon had yet to determine how much she knew of her late husband's activities. He had no doubt Deverell had some incriminating document, much like the one Malvina clutched in one small fist. If she thought Deverell would trade, she was in for a rude shock.

He placed one hand over her fist. The other she had clutched in her nightdress. Barely squeezing, he felt the delicate bones of her fingers grinding together.

She continued to stare at him, tears forming in her eyes even as she bit her lower lip. He could see her determination not to cry and her realization of the futility of resisting his greater strength.

He studied her lips, overcome with a sudden longing to kiss her. He resisted the urge, believing, quite truthfully, that he would lose in the end.

Malvina whimpered. He was hurting her and it was hurting him. Throwing caution to the winds, he released her hand and leaned forward, closing the distance between their mouths.

At first contact, she jumped. Then she sighed and leaned in, forgetting everything but the wonderful touch of his lips. Her fingers loosened and she barely noticed the document slipping from her fingers to fall, unheeded, to the floor.

Reaching up, she touched him, fleetingly, a bare stroking of his cheek. He rose, cradling her in his arms. He never broke the contact of their lips.

It was several moments before he became aware that his face was wet with her tears. He released her mouth, realizing the document had dropped from her fingers. He kicked it under the chair and sat down on it, settling her comfortably on his lap.

He brushed the tears away with his thumbs and saw the way her throat worked, as if she tried to speak but was prevented by strong emotion. "You can tell me. I want to protect you but you have to trust me."

"It was y-you," she managed to stutter. Taking a deep breath, she successfully forced the sobs back. "He said he would kill *you*."

Shock rendered him silent. His face went blank, his eyes full of all sorts of thoughts. She read surprise, awe, and utter amazement. And somewhere in the back, buried beneath the other emotions, she ascertained horror.

She felt bereft when his lids drooped, hiding himself from her. It was the thing she hated about him, the lazy, care-for-nothing expression that closed off the rest of the world.

She pushed herself away. In revealing how upset she was at the threat to his life, she had also revealed how attached she had become. And Gideon, dratted man that he was, just sat there, silent.

Standing on legs that threatened to buckle beneath her, Malvina told him, "I will leave you now, my lord. You have successfully gotten what you wanted from me. I applaud you."

He stood, catching her hand as she swung away. "I did not get *everything* I wanted."

She pulled free. "I am in no mood for your games, Lord Holt. You have achieved what you wanted with your callousness. The document is yours. I will take my chances with your...*friend*."

"He is no friend of mine and I need you to give him that document. He expects that I do not know enough of your activities with him to take him in. I need him to continue to believe that."

Malvina stared at the document Gideon tossed at her feet. Her gaze slid up to meet his. "You want me to give this to him?"

"Yes."

"Why? Is this not what you have been looking for? The way to prove Deverell is a traitor?"

"To be honest, the one we want includes your husband's name."

Her mouth dropped. She was frozen for three full seconds. Then, she moved so quickly, he didn't see her coming.

She slapped him with the full force of her body behind the blow. His head snapped back, a ringing starting almost immediately in his ears.

"Deceiver," she snarled. "Liar. Scoundrel!"

If she hadn't been so righteously—and rightly—angry, Gideon would have smiled. Or kissed her. Perhaps both. She was passionately beautiful, all flaming hair, heaving bosom, and flushed skin.

Slightly alarmed by his own overly dramatic musings, he attempted to diffuse the situation.

"Were my lies any worse than yours?"

She stalked to the door. Just when he thought she would leave, she turned and stalked back. She stood before him, fists on her hips.

Shaking a finger in his face, she informed him hotly, "I was trying to protect my son. I was trying to prevent him from discovering exactly what his father was. Not to mention the fact that when it is proven that he was a traitor, we will lose everything. We will be hounded from Society, ostracized."

"I can prevent that," he murmured.

Stepping back—she had nearly been standing on his toes—she gave him a suspicious look. "How? I was under the impression that miracles are not of man but God."

A funny little smile played across his lips. "Found my book, did you?" He shrugged. "I have eccentric tastes in literature."

She shook her head impatiently. "I will not be distracted. How can you save us?"

Gideon took her hands and pulled her close. "I proposed marriage for a reason, Malvina. I suspected the truth from the start. Why else would you risk everything?" He placed both hands on her face, drawing her closer still, forcing her to meet his gaze. "I knew of your innocence from the moment I rescued you from the *highwaymen*. Despite everything I have ever said to you, I never thought you were willingly doing what Deverell wanted."

"Why did you never say anything?" she asked calmly, finding his gentle touch a wonderful substitute for the indifference she'd come to expect from her late husband.

Pausing for a long, drawn-out moment, he finally replied, "I wanted you to tell me. Silly of me to wish for such a thing when you distrusted me as you did."

Malvina closed the last few inches that separated them, forcing him to close his arms around her. They stood for a moment, each one lost in thought and the wonderful sensation of simply being held.

The mantel clock chimed midnight. Malvina jumped, knocking her head into Gideon's chin. His teeth clacked together, causing him to curse. Malvina stifled a giggle and moved away from him.

"It is exceedingly late," she murmured. "I should be off."

Gideon gave her a look that she vaguely recognized. It had been years since she'd seen such an expression.

His words confirmed it. "You don't have to leave."

Tempted far more than she cared to admit, she nevertheless declined his offer. She was infinitely thankful that he kept his distance. Had he touched her again, she would not have been able to resist. With that thought firmly in the forefront of her mind, she fled to her own chamber.

15

Wolf's insides churned every time he thought about it. It was all he could do to keep the contents of his stomach where they belonged.

He had witnessed his mother leaving Lord Holt's chamber practically in the middle of the night like a common trollop. While he was not hypocritical enough to believe his father deserved her loyalty even after death, he still felt she should have some self-respect.

It had not helped that this very morning, before anyone had risen from their beds, he had chanced to see his mother meeting another man in a clandestine manner. He had seen them at the old folly, not far from where Wolf had been walking to clear his head. He recognized the man from church. Why would his mother be meeting him?

Wolf marched to the stables at an ungodly hour, the sun just rising from its own bed. He needed to escape for a time. There were too many petticoats present for his comfort and he was becoming too attached to Lady Samantha de Witt. She was not for him. No lady was.

He did not wait for a groom to ready a mount. He saddled one himself. He didn't even realize which one he'd selected until he mounted. It was Black, one of Holt's personal hunters. It was the very beast that had traveled with them to Yorkshire, tied behind the carriage that conveyed Holt, Wolf, and Malvina.

The earl's horses all had such stupid names.

Wolf didn't care. He galloped from the stable yard with little regard for human or animal life. He headed straight for the relative loneliness of the moors. He did not notice the beauty of the heather; he did not notice the threat of the bogs.

It didn't take long for Wolf to gallop off the majority of the rage, disgust, and disappointment he felt. He slowed to a walk, paying little attention to his surroundings.

Life wasn't fair, he reflected. Being born into a wealthy family with a title, even a meager one, was supposed to be, on some level, a privilege. Sir Beowulf Brackney had trouble looking at his life with anything more than grim disbelief.

Black stumbled. Wolf steadied him without thought, not realizing he was wandering through a rocky area he'd never ridden with Samantha.

The late Sir Richard Brackney had been, at best, an indifferent parent. He had taken pride in little that his son had done. The few things he'd noticed in a positive way were not things for which a child should be praised.

Wolf had played terrible, cruel tricks on the housemaids and other children. His father had laughed and complimented his ingenuity.

It was his mother who prevented Wolf from falling completely under the influence of his sire. It was her gentle disapproval, her loving concern, and never failing pride in his true accomplishments that had held him together.

All appearances to the contrary, Wolf loved his mother. To see her selling herself to Lord Holt for protection made him feel physically ill. She deserved so much better.

Black stumbled again. The poor beast was trying to pick his way around a rocky outcropping and having little success. Wolf glanced around, concerned. He had not realized just how far he'd ridden or exactly where he was.

He carefully turned Black, who gratefully followed the direction. He seemed more comfortable, knowing his way home.

It was this self-assurance on the horse's part that was Wolf's downfall. Just when the manor came into view and Wolf released a sigh of relief, Black tripped.

The young baronet was thrown, striking his shoulder painfully on a boulder. He fought for consciousness, forcing the pain into the back recesses of his mind. It was a useful trick his father had taught him during the few times he'd decided to teach him anything.

With the pain under control, Wolf was able to take stock of his situation. He emitted a low groan when he saw Black. The poor creature lay on his side, whinnying pitifully. One glance told Wolf that the gelding's leg was broken.

Feeling an unmanly urge to cry, Wolf slowly rose, favoring his right side from neck to waist. He moved to Black's side and crouched down, brushing his hand over the animal's heaving shoulder.

Stupid beast, anyway. Black should have known this area. What horse doesn't know where not to step?

Cursing, he stood. There was nothing he could do for the animal. He was only sixteen. He was not in the habit of carrying a pistol. Unfortunately, that was the only help left for Black.

His trek back to the house was fraught with the urge to run in the opposite direction and never return. He messed up again and he did not look forward to whatever punishment the earl felt was appropriate for killing his horse.

Malvina saw him coming. She had spent hours searching for him, intent on telling him they were to leave for London early the following morning.

After returning from her morning meeting with Lord Delwyn, at which she'd handed over the document as ordered, the earl had confided his need to speak with his superiors at the Home Office. A little relieved to be able to leave, Malvina had readily agreed.

She ventured outside again, not sure what drew her attention to the north. On the edge of the park, she could see the figure of her son, cradling his right shoulder. He stumbled as she watched, and almost fell.

She drew in a sharp breath. Her heart constricted and jumped into her throat. When Wolf fell to his knees, she screamed.

Malvina didn't even realize she was running until she tripped, tearing her skirts and scraping her leg. She pushed herself back to her feet and kept on.

She couldn't form a coherent thought as she ran. All she could see was her child hurt, broken.

"Wolf!"

He looked up. His blue eyes shimmered with tears and Malvina felt her own fill up. She had not seen her son cry since he was but a boy. He hadn't even shed a tear the night his father died.

She fell to her knees beside him, reaching for him. "Wolf, what happened?"

"I was thrown."

"Are you hurt? What happened to your arm?"

"My shoulder is bruised," he told her, rolling the appendage with a grimace of pain. "I hit a rock."

Relieved that his injuries seemed minor, she allowed her tension to ease a bit. Her relief was short-lived, however, when she realized his horse was missing. A shiver of unease consumed her. "Where is the horse?"

A single tear escaped. "He is back there," Wolf said, tipping his head in the direction from which he'd come.

"Oh, Wolf, what have you done?"

People arrived. Servants, stable hands, and family rushed to them, everyone asking questions at once and demanding answers.

Lady Samantha flopped down beside her friend and tried to take his hand. He resisted her touch, an action that alarmed Malvina more than it should have. The young lady, however, merely shrugged and continued to sit beside him, offering her undemanding support.

Malvina felt Gideon's presence behind her. He stooped down and looked the boy over, grunting when he was satisfied that Wolf would survive.

"Why would you ride over terrain you do not know?" he asked, his voice laced with a concern that Wolf had only ever received from his mother.

"I wasn't thinking," he admitted, confused by the solicitude of this man. "I was angry."

"Where is your mount?" Gideon looked up at the stable master. "Has the beast returned home?"

"Nay, milord," ventured the man hesitantly. "The young master took Black."

Gideon's face froze. He speared the hapless Wolf with hard eyes. "Where is Black?"

Samantha leaned away from him, her soft brown eyes unusually hard. "Why do they have such stupid names?" Wolf blurted unwisely, his guilt and embarrassment speaking.

"Where is Black?"

Malvina saw her son's miserable expression mingle with a look that heralded a loss of temper. She spoke up, seeking to avoid bloodshed.

"Back that way, Gideon."

Wolf was man enough to meet Gideon's eyes as the older man straightened. The earl said nothing and held out his hand. A pistol, primed and ready to fire, was slapped into his palm.

For a heart-stopping second, Malvina thought he meant to use the weapon on her son. She opened her mouth to object, positioned herself to shield her child, but ended by saying nothing as Gideon stalked off.

Minutes later—it felt like hours—a gunshot was heard. Malvina wrapped her arms around Wolf and he buried his face in her neck, reminding her painfully of the child he once was. They all waited on tenterhooks, apprehension a palpable entity.

The stable hands moved in the direction of the shot, knowing it would be their task to take care of Black's remains. They each tugged their forelock as the earl came past, the stable master receiving the spent weapon.

Malvina watched Gideon move, her heart wrenching at the pain she saw in his eyes. He glanced at her once, accusingly, but never slowed. They watched him go, unsurprised when he veered off to the stables.

Samantha stood, her movements a little less graceful than usual. Tears stood out in her eyes, her scarred visage flushed. "That was very bad of you, Wolf. Giddy has few attachments. Black was the one above all others."

She stepped carefully around him, holding her skirts away as if he was diseased. "I will bid you adieu now, Lady Malvina, Sir Beowulf. Have an uneventful journey."

His forehead creased in confusion, Wolf shrugged out of his mother's embrace. "What in hell is Sam talking about?"

Malvina winced. "Language, darling." She reached out to smooth a lock of dark red hair from his brow. He flinched away as if she were about to strike him.

Her hand dropped, a forlorn expression touching her delicate features. "I am so sorry for everything, Wolf," she whispered. "I should have helped you when—"

"There was nothing you could do, Mother," he interrupted, not willing to have the discussion she wanted. He stood, unwillingly allowing his mother to help. "I did what I had to, eventually. The matter is not to be mentioned again."

A little stunned by the adult she could see in the eyes of her baby, all Malvina could do was nod. She put her arm through his and together, they moved to the house, the two of them against the world.

As usual.

# 16

They left the following morning. Lady Samantha had already said her goodbyes to the Brackneys and only appeared to tell her brother to be safe. He hesitated for a moment before drawing her to him and embracing her warmly.

"I'll miss you, Sammy. Take care of Mother."

"Do not stay away so long this time, Giddy. This mausoleum is not the same without you."

He smiled. "Hardly that, Sam." He saw the yearning in her eyes and promised, "I will send for you to come to us for the Season. If you still want one."

"Of course I do." Her brow furrowed. "Us?"

His eyebrows rose. "I will be married by then. Naturally, your visit will be with my wife and I. And her son."

"You will still marry Lady Malvina?"

Gideon glanced to the carriage where his betrothed and his soon-to-be stepson were waiting. Nodding, he turned back to this sister. "I will. What Wolf did was stupid and thoughtless and ended badly. But he needs a father more than I needed Black."

Samantha's lips trembled. "Do you think you can help him?"

"I hope so."

"Mama and I cannot attend your wedding?" Her tone suggested hurt.

Gideon shook his head. "Do you believe Mama would? She refused to say goodbye because she is angry I even brought Malvina here. As much as I would love to have you there, it will not do."

"And there is that other business you have to finish," Samantha said, her clear brown eyes indicating her knowledge of more than was safe for her to know. "I never did trust Lord Delwyn, Giddy. He is oily, like a toad. Do be careful."

"Toads are not oily."

Samantha rolled her eyes at her brother. "You know what I mean. He's sneaky and untrustworthy."

"You know nothing, Sammy," he said implacably. "Stay out of trouble and select a good mount for Wolf. It is to be our gift to him."

She was visibly shocked. "You would give him a horse after what he did to Black? It is all well and good trying to save him from himself, Giddy, but to allow him to hurt another animal is just...just—"

He stopped her, gently taking her hand. "He will learn to care for something other than himself. He is spoiled and selfish and bitterly angry. He needs responsibility." At her continued look of disbelief, he added, "I will watch him, Sam. Do not fret."

Lady Malvina and her son watched the two as they spoke. "What is she telling him, do you think?" Wolf asked.

"Nothing to concern us," his mother said automatically.

Wolf snorted. "Sure," he scoffed. "She is probably convincing him to murder us along the road."

"He will not agree," Malvina murmured, not denying the possibility of Samantha's words.

"I would not blame him at all if he did," her son reluctantly confided in an undertone.

Malvina sat mum for several seconds. Then, "Why did you do it, Wolf?"

He shrugged and turned his face away. She thought he would not reply when he muttered, "I saw you leave his room."

Her fingers spasmed in her lap. "You did?" He nodded. "Well, I am sure you are mature enough to realize your mother is a grown woman, free to remarry."

He grunted. "You are not married, Mother. Just because you are engaged does not mean he has the right to treat you as his doxy."

Her face flamed. "Language, Wolf," she remonstrated. "Your father would not begrudge me another chance at happiness."

She jumped at the short bark of laughter her son felt compelled to release. "That is rich, Mother! Father would come back and beat you if he wasn't licking Satan's boots in hell."

Donning the sternest expression she could muster, she said, "I know your feelings for your father are not of the fondest. But he is dead now and deserves forgiveness for his sins."

Wolf just looked at her. His expression was completely blank, blue eyes devoid of emotion. In a frighteningly steady voice, he told her, "Father has not paid nearly enough for his sins. He can burn in hell for a thousand lifetimes and still not pay for his sins."

She surprised him. "I'm not at all sure anyone *burns* in hell, my love."

He sat back, refusing to enter into a debate with her.

Lady Malvina released the breath she didn't realize she was holding. Gideon kissed his sister on the cheek and moved to the coach. He stepped in and sat beside Malvina in the forward facing seat.

He didn't smile or give any indication that he'd forgiven Wolf for Black's death. He didn't even glance Malvina's way. He simply rapped on the roof with his stick.

"Do we travel straight through?" Malvina ventured cautiously.

"No, indeed. I am a gentleman, after all."

His response was not satisfying in the least, but she saw the wisdom in allowing him some peace. Black's death had affected him greatly.

"Why the names?"

"What names?" Gideon murmured, his voice taking on the lazy shield he donned when feeling threatened.

"The dam... dashed horses. Why do you choose such nonsensical monikers?"

Inwardly, Malvina groaned at her imprudent son's query. Could he not have chosen a more sensible subject? Better yet, why could he not have kept his mouth firmly shut?

Gideon slouched in his seat, tipping his hat forward to shade his eyes. "They all have eminently suitable names. The brown horse is Brown, the gray horse Gray, the black horse..."

There was a moment of uncomfortable silence. Then, "What if you have more than one color?"

"Wolf!"

Gideon pushed his hat back, meeting the younger man's eyes. "What do you think I call them? I do have another black horse."

Malvina opened her mouth. "Black Two."

He smiled. "Eminently suitable." So saying, he settled deeper into the seat and again pulled his hat down.

They reached London several days later. Settling his "almost family" into his townhouse in Berkeley Square, he left immediately, his destination Doctors Commons to procure a special license from the Archbishop of Canterbury. He was determined to have that situation well in hand before Deverell could make mischief. Or anyone else for that matter.

It was well he'd had the foresight to apply for a license long before. The seven day waiting period was past so he knew all he had to do was fetch it. Even Lord Byron had had to wait seven days for his special license.

He had a few more stops to make, and if all went as planned, he would be well and truly married to a beautiful creature who had far more to offer than she believed.

17

Malvina settled in quite well but knew she was courting disaster by staying in the home of her betrothed. She was a widow and could take advantage of more freedom but Society would only forgive so much. Thankfully, Town was rather sparse of company at the moment.

That would only last a few more weeks, Malvina thought. She wasn't sure how long Gideon planned for their engagement to stand. If it was longer than a week or two, her reputation would be thoroughly ruined.

She sighed. Once it was known that her late husband was a traitor to the crown, her reputation would be for naught anyway.

She stood at the drawing room window, watching the traffic outside. Gideon had left as soon as they arrived, citing appointments he could not miss. Naturally, she was curious, but still felt she should keep her distance.

Wolf was out walking. She had not wanted him to go out alone as it was his first visit to London, but he had insisted, confiding that it was not *his* first visit.

Apparently, when he was supposed to be staying with Deveraux Ashby, heir to the Marquis of Preston, he and Deveraux had been in London learning to be *men*. They had spent entire holidays in Town, their parents blissfully unaware that their precious babies were trying to grow up.

Malvina did not know her son at all.

The door opened and Malvina turned. A maid entered, curtsied. "Would you care for tea, milady?"

"Yes, thank you," she smiled.

With another curtsy, the maid left, a curious but not insolent look on her pretty features. Malvina wondered at it. The servants had been introduced upon their arrival and they had all been everything that was proper. Lady Malvina could only assume they had not heard of her husband or her lowly birth.

Turning back to the window, Malvina saw Wolf return. She could not see him well; his hat shielded much of his features from her motherly gaze. He glanced up at the window briefly and she gasped.

With one eye swollen shut, the cheek beneath cut and oozing blood, a split lip, an ugly bruise darkening his jaw, and one arm clutching the shoulder he'd already injured once, he looked like a grotesque gargoyle come to life.

A curse slipped out just as the maid returned with tea. The girl gasped, the items on her tray clattering together. The sound brought her mistress swinging round.

"Oh, Mary, you startled me." She laughed. "I must have startled you as well. Here, you may place the tray on the table." When the maid left, Malvina followed her out.

She met Wolf in the corridor. He ducked his head and tried to move past her.

She laid her hand on his uninjured arm. "Are you well?"

Her gentle voice belied the churning fear that consumed her. Every day that passed took her only child that much more from her; eventually, he would leave her and she was terrified she would never see him again. He was heading for a bad end, as the saying went.

Wolf smiled, an odd sort of smile filled with contentment and...life. It was not an expression she'd ever seen on his face before.

"I am well, Mother. Merely a scrap at the docks."

"What were you doing at the docks? It's dangerous there."

"You don't say?"

"Sarcasm ill becomes you, young sir."

They turned to see the earl had returned from his errands. He handed his hat and stick to the footman. With a lazy smile, he ushered them into the drawing room, shushing Wolf when that young gentleman tried to object.

"We have several things to discuss," Gideon told them.

He solicitously seated Malvina, then turned to Wolf. "What is the extent of your injuries?"

"I'm not sure," he admitted. "My shoulder is worse but I think a few ribs are broken, as well."

"May I?"

Wolf nodded, straightening his arm to allow the earl to poke and prod at him. Gideon was pleased to note the injuries were mostly superficial. "We need to bind your ribs. Who rescued you?"

The younger man frowned. "Why do you assume I was rescued?"

His query met with silence. Then, "Who?"

"Some stranger in black."

Gideon had been about to turn away but something in Wolf's tone stopped him. "Black?"

"Oddest fellow. His clothes were black but so was his hair. He jumped right in and pummeled two of the three nearly to death. I managed to take the third out and the fourth ran off. It was glorious!"

"Glorious?" Malvina whispered, her face unnaturally white. "Glorious!"

The gentlemen had forgotten her presence. Wolf flushed and Gideon cursed, but Malvina ignored that. Rising, she rounded on her son.

"You were beaten nearly to death and all you can do is praise some ruffian and call it all glorious?"

A snicker from Gideon attracted her fulminating glare. "What is so funny?"

He rubbed his finger along his eye. "Hart would enjoy being called a ruffian, I think." His lips twitched suspiciously but he didn't laugh again.

"Hart?"

"Hartley St. Clair, Duke of Derringer, Lord Heartless. I think I have even heard him called the Devil Incarnate but I don't give that rumor much credence."

Wolf's expression turned to one of awe, reminding his companions that, appearances to the contrary, he was still little more than a child.

"The Duke of Derringer? Truly? How do you know?"

Gideon snorted and moved to Malvina's side. "He never really was in any real danger, my love. If it was indeed Derringer, he was there the entire time. He would never have allowed Wolf to be seriously hurt."

She allowed the earl to help her back to her seat but she was not so easily cajoled out of her indignation. "Why would he not?"

Gideon sat beside her and took her hand. "He would know who Wolf was the moment the boy stepped into view. There is nothing Hart does not know or quickly discover. He will know the answer to my question, I'm sure."

"How do you find him?"

Gideon looked at the young baronet with a measuring glance. "I do believe you are the answer to that very question, my lad. We will use you as bait."

Malvina's fingers tightened on his. "Bait?"

"Calm, love. He'll not be injured again. Wolf will merely serve to bring the elusive duke out of hiding."

"Do you suspect him of treason?" Malvina asked.

"Good Lord, no! Whatever gave you that idea?"

Her forehead creased. "Why is he in hiding and behaving so oddly if he is not involved in something nefarious?"

"Oh, I am sure his activities are nefarious but never treasonous," Gideon told her on a laugh. "As for his reasons for playing at villain, he is most likely bored. He finds the duties of the duchy tedious in the extreme."

"I am not sure I want my son associating with such a man," Malvina ventured, still frowning.

The gentlemen in her life gave her such a look of disgust that she felt the color rising in her cheeks. "Why do you look so? Is it not normal for a mother to desire her son to form healthy connections?"

"Hart did save his life," Gideon pointed out reasonably. "I would not think there could be anything better said in his favor."

She had to allow that. However, "Wolf should not have been at the docks in the first place."

"I am still present," said that young man, annoyed.

A lazy grin touched Gideon's lips. "So you are. Fancy that." He promptly ignored him again, turning back to the boy's mother. "The bottom line is, Hart can point me in the right direction to uncovering the truth of your husband's involvement with Deverell." He paused, his deep thoughts mirrored in his eyes. "He always said, even in school, that Deverell was no good."

Malvina shook her head and turned her pale green eyes on her son, "Go make yourself presentable, Wolf. I need to speak with Gideon."

The boy hesitated but after a bland look from the earl, he snorted and left, without so much as a bow for his mother.

"Thoughtless," murmured Gideon to no one in particular. "Do you feel up to socializing this week?"

Malvina glanced at the tea things and offered to send for more, assuming correctly that it was less than lukewarm. Gideon rang the bellpull and returned to her side, taking her hand again in a clasp that was casual and possessive all at once.

Staring at their linked hands, Malvina felt unaccountable tears come to her eyes and wondered if she was sickening for something. Since she had met Gideon, her feelings had been in an uproar. Nothing made sense anymore, which wasn't saying much considering her life had always been rather dramatic. Being married to a man who was constantly involving himself in matters he shouldn't had lent a flair to her life that she hadn't appreciated. Would marrying a spy-hunting earl make things any better?

Deep down, Malvina craved peace. She wanted the most exciting thing in her life to be which bonnet to wear with which pelisse. Or how much money was required to install a new closed range in the kitchen. Wondering if her son would be killed wandering London's East End or her betrothed would be shot while unraveling a conspiracy against the crown or her late husband would be revealed as a traitor was not a pleasant feeling.

A maid entered with all the efficiency of a well-trained servant and was bidden to fetch new tea. Seconds after arriving, she was gone again.

Pushing aside her morose longings, Malvina focused her thoughts on the topic introduced. "Where did you desire to go?" she asked, referring to his earlier question.

"Only to the theater," he said. Letting go of her hand, he moved his arm and rested it along the sofa back. "There is a pretty bird there who I am told is worth seeing." He reached out with his free hand and fingered a curl near her cheek, his eyes roving over her face like a caress.

She wanted to ask who the pretty bird was but the chills she felt down her spine prevented speech. Why did a fleeting touch of his fingers cause such odd sensations?

"We have not discussed our upcoming nuptials," he said, his warm breath on her cheek.

She turned to look at him. She realized her mistake almost immediately. His lips were mere inches from hers and closing in.

Malvina knew she should move. She did not want him to kiss her. She did not want to feel this fluttery feeling, this excited anticipation and longing for something she should not desire. She should not desire this man with the piercing, revealing gaze who was four years her junior. It was not right.

She didn't move. The hand by her cheek moved around her neck and drew her closer. He paused there to say, "We marry tonight." He kissed her before she could breathe, let alone speak.

The rush of emotion that went through Malvina in that moment was indescribable. Shock, excitement, anger, fear, and pure unadulterated lust were only a few. Her brain could not select just one to feel so she continued to feel them all.

Until her undeniable attraction to the man in her arms took over. Her hands slid up over his shoulders and into his dark blond hair as she kissed him back, putting all that she had into the embrace, and for the first time in her life, she felt hope.

And she cried. The tears squeezed through her eyelids, slowly, calmly, as if she were not overcome with emotion at all.

Lord Holt shifted, his hands framing her face, a look of tender concern and a little bit of chagrin on his handsome features. "That was not the reaction, or the reply, I was hoping for, my love."

His thumbs brushed away the tears and Malvina's control returned. She sniffled, accepting the handkerchief thrust under her nose.

Mopping her face, she said pertly, "I was not aware I had a choice."

He smoothed a few dark red strands of silky hair back from her face. "No, perhaps you don't."

Malvina shook her head. "I was married once to a man who could not love me. I'll not do that again."

"Brackney was a fool."

Hardly daring to believe the words she'd just heard, she opened her mouth to demand an explanation. The opening of the door forestalled her words, revealing the tea tray and Wolf.

He gave them a look of patent disgust, their position next to each other rather self-explanatory. "Tea is here," he said unnecessarily, gesturing to the tea things as if they were the ones to have offended his young sensibilities.

Malvina poured, pondering all that had happened while listening to the two most important people in her life speak of matters she'd rather know nothing about. She did not want to hear them make plans to bring the Duke of Derringer out of hiding. Even if the man had saved Wolf, he was quite obviously attics to let and therefore, dangerous.

A sharp bark of dark laughter ripped her from her musings. Looking to the door, she saw a filthy, ragged beast of a man filling the portal. Her face flamed. She had not realized she'd spoken aloud. "I am sorry. That was dreadfully rude."

The gentlemen rose slowly to their feet, as if unable to believe the sight that met their eyes. Wolf stepped forward, suddenly all eagerness to officially meet the infamous "Lord Heartless."

"You were simply marvelous, sir. Bloody damn magnificent! Where did you learn to fight like that?"

"Language," the dirty man muttered. Glancing at Gideon, he asked, "Who is the puppy, Witless?"

Gideon's eyebrows rose ever so slightly. "I did ask you once to remind me to call you out, did I not? Reminder taken. It will have to be next week, however. I am getting married tonight."

A lascivious grin turned the other man's face into something Malvina found to be quite unnerving. She suppressed a shudder.

Their visitor gave her a cursory glance, saying rather perfunctorily, "Congratulations. A lusty wench, I'm sure."

Jamieson, Holt's butler in London, entered just after the duke, his face flushed with anxiety. "I beg your pardon, milord, but this person simply walked past as if he lives here."

"Where are you staying?" the earl asked rhetorically, waving off the concern of Jamieson. When that faithful retainer hesitated, Lord Holt told him patiently, "You are commended for not setting the footmen on him. I do hate how blood stains."

On that cryptic remark, Jamieson fled.

Gideon gestured for the duke to enter, saying, "A word of caution: You may call me what you will, Hart, but one thing inappropriate or insulting to Lady Malvina and I will kill you where you stand."

Malvina was on her feet before she'd realized that she'd moved. "Violence is unnecessary, my lords, truly." Turning, she bid the duke to join them for tea. "You are Lord Derringer, I believe. I must say I am pleased you have suddenly appeared. Now Wolf will not have to lure you out."

Her ingenuous remark was met with another sharp laugh. He moved further into the room, looking her up and down with a glance that was both insolent and insulting. He glanced at Lord Holt before favoring her with a wholly inappropriate leer.

Malvina laughed. She was not sure why, but something in the duke's actions reminded her greatly of a boy provoking a response from a rival. It warmed her heart in an odd sort of way. She had seen her son and his friend Deveraux act in just such a manner.

"Oh, I take it all back, Witless." Bowing before Malvina, Derringer added, "If I were not so hellbent on bachelorhood, I would steal you away."

Something in Malvina clenched. This man was not at all what she would want in a husband. And yet...

And yet, there was a magnetism about him that was impossible to explain. Or ignore.

The devilish light that entered his eyes at that moment snapped her out of her reverie. It was unconscionable that she think in such a way about this man to whom she'd only just been introduced. Worse yet, to do so in front of her betrothed!

She glanced at Gideon, part of her wondering if he would lose his temper, slap her, tell her she was disloyal, a whore. Memories feathered the edges of her vision but she refused to allow them entrance.

The earl rolled his eyes at the duke. "Hart, she is not so easily seduced. She does at least require that her lovers be...*clean.*"

Eyebrows rising at the implication inherent in Gideon's words, Malvina offered curtly, "Not so, my lord. I only require that they be"—she paused significantly, eyeing each gentleman as insultingly as she could—"older."

Derringer's mouth split into a wide grin, his eyes dancing with an unholy light. "I can understand your obsession with this one, Witless," he remarked over his shoulder. "She would make many a man eager to break her to saddle."

"Hart!"

Raising his eyes to the lady's son, the duke added, "You may want to be aware that her child will try to murder you sooner or later."

He stepped away from the lady and sat, not bothering to wait for Lady Malvina to do so first. He ignored the growl that came from the direction of the boy, gazing around him as if he'd never seen his friend's home before.

"I like what you've done with this barn, Witless. Much more personable."

Gideon looked up at the ceiling as if entreating God for the patience to deal with his eccentric friend. "You have no idea how pleased I am to hear you say so," he drawled.

Malvina had heard quite enough. The duke was odd, possibly dangerous, and she had no desire to witness any more of their exchange.

With a slight curtsy, she bid the gentlemen good evening and prepared to leave. Gideon stopped her before she'd taken two steps.

"We marry in two hours, my love. The Jamiesons will stand witness."

# 204 — Jaimey Grant

Her knees nearly gave out. "Two hours?"

A muffled snort came from the duke's direction but when she glanced at him, his expression was innocence personified. Gideon tossed a disgruntled look the other man's way.

Wolf chose that moment to remind the adults that he was still present.

"Two hours? Are you bloody daft?"

"Language!" three adults said at once.

"Although," the duke added reflectively, "it is only due to your mother's presence that we object. If she would make good on her threat to leave, your language would not be out of place."

"I do not believe gentlemen should ever speak so," Malvina retorted, wondering why this man managed to annoy her far more than any other man. Perhaps it was fear?

Derringer leveled a blank stare on her. "Are you leaving?"

"Of all the...! You, sir, are abominably rude!"

He laughed. The wretched creature actually laughed. Malvina took a deep breath. "Young man, you need a lesson in manners."

Derringer's face darkened. Gideon groaned, stepping quickly between the two. Facing his affianced, he muttered, "Are you trying to get yourself killed?"

Her shock was not feigned. "He is your friend. And rude."

"He is also unbalanced, Malvina. Tread carefully."

Leaning a little to the left, she could see the duke where he still sat, his whole body coiled and tensed, as if awaiting attack. She bit her lip, meeting Gideon's eyes.

"Can we help him?"

"We do not know what is wrong with him." He leaned forward and kissed her lightly on the forehead, ignoring the sound of vexation that emerged from her son. "Go now, love. Leave us to plot like the villains we are."

She stared at him long and hard, finally nodding, defeated. "Very well. Wolf, come."

"Oh, mummy-dearest," mocked the duke, "please let him stay and play? We need to pick his innocent brain."

The fear that streaked through Malvina widened her green eyes and stopped her heart. She opened her mouth to object.

"Hart, you fool. Why would any mother trust you with her precious son when you act as though you are only fit for Bedlam?"

Derringer grinned, his white teeth flashing incongruously against his soot-blackened skin. "I have been to Bethlehem Hospital, my friend. It is paradise compared to some places I've seen."

Again addressing Lady Malvina, with far more respect than before, he added, "No harm will come to your child, my lady. We need to steer him aright if you want to keep him alive."

"Here now!" Wolf inserted, insulted.

They ignored him.

"You, my lord of the Rookeries, believe you are capable of doing this?" A grim smile touched her lips. "How can you save him when you have so clearly failed to save yourself?"

One second later, Malvina found herself standing outside the drawing room, staring at the closed door.

18

"She meant nothing, Hart. Calm yourself."

The most noble Duke of Derringer was fit to be tied. His demeanor alarmed Gideon, who had never witnessed a complete loss of control in this particular man. He raved and paced the room, as if seeking some object on which to direct his rage.

Gideon prayed Wolf was wise enough to keep silent. In fact...

"Get out, Wolf. Now."

Shockingly, the boy did as he was told, immediately quitting the room. Gideon watched him go, catching a glimpse of Malvina still standing on the other side. Her eyes were wide with fright, and haunted by an emotion that went much deeper.

He shook it off. The door closed again, giving Gideon the chance to use whatever means necessary to calm his friend. Lord, if ever there was a time he needed Levi Greville, Derringer's best friend, it was now.

But Levi was occupied with his new family. Derringer was Gideon's problem now.

Stepping as close as he dared, he tried to reach him with words. Derringer lunged, Gideon recoiled, reacting without thought. He struck out, hitting the duke on the jaw.

Derringer went down, briefly. He came back up, murder in his eyes. Lord Holt backed away, his hands raised defensively as Derringer worked his jaw back and forth.

"See reason, Hart. Women speak nonsense all the time. They are not to be taken seriously."

"This one crossed the line, Witless."

Gideon's hands dropped. He sighed. "Why must you insist on calling me that? It is a most demoralizing appellation."

"Hence, the reason I use it."

"Are you again the well-bred English gentleman that I know is in there somewhere?"

"Only if I ate him," Derringer scoffed. "A brandy would not come amiss." The earl moved to comply with the duke's request.

He stared at Lord Holt. "How bad was it?"

Gideon paused in the act of filling two tumblers with the jewel-toned spirits he favored. He closed his eyes briefly, not glancing up.

Finishing his task, he turned, handing one glass to the other man. "Do you not remember?"

"There are times.... I don't know what comes over me." He quaffed the liquid in his glass, staring into the nothingness left behind. He silently held it out.

Gideon complied with the unspoken request, offering, "You were right about Deverell, Hart."

The duke snorted. "Of course I was right. You doubted me?"

Jerking his head slightly in agreement, he said, "You are not easy to believe, my friend. If it were not for your mad starts, one would listen without conscious thought. You, however, discount your warnings with a new scandal, intrigue, or threat."

This pronouncement caused the duke to shrug, unconcerned. "If everyone heeded my dire predictions, life would become very dull indeed."

"Why the devil did you not report to the Home Office when you learned of Deverell's activities?"

Derringer's look was almost pitying. He moved to set his newly emptied glass on the side table. "I do not put myself out to do anyone a favor, Witless. That includes the government."

"You told me."

"I stumbled upon the knowledge and gave it to someone I knew was involved in Prinny's dirty work. That was as far as I was or am willing to go."

"I need proof, Hart."

"You have proof, or did, at one time. Did you give in to his blackmail, then?"

"Of course I did. He feels he can have Brackney convicted of treason."

"The man's dead," Derringer pointed out reasonably. "What real hold does Deverell have?"

"They can still lose everything should the government wish to take it. Even then, all of Society will condemn them. Treason affects everyone."

Derringer picked up a little Dresden figurine. He examined it minutely before stowing it away in one capacious pocket of his moth-eaten coat. Gideon said nothing, knowing full well that the duke would deny ever stealing a thing. And Gideon would probably end up believing him.

"You have wealth enough," the duke pointed out, holding up an enamel snuffbox. He added it to his newly acquired possessions with an unrepentant grin.

"Brackney was a baronet."

"Do the boy a good turn, then, Witless. Take the title and let him be himself."

"Not all view the responsibility of a title with such loathing."

"Be that as it may, your young puppy is not desirous of his duties. He wants freedom. Freedom from his father."

Lord Holt refilled his own brandy glass, two fingers worth, quaffing it immediately. He grimaced at the burn but felt the need for it.

Derringer was a trying fellow in the best of times. When he was blatantly larcenous and argumentative, he was impossible.

"We will not get into that. I do not want Malvina going through the inevitable scandal."

The duke leveled a stern gaze on him. "And in protecting her *good name* you have opened yourself up to charges of treason. Is she worth it?"

"Yes."

Derringer's black brows shot up. "Indeed? Is that how it is, then? I pity you, you fool."

He moved to leave, having helped himself to the countess's favorite silver candlesticks.

"What the devil are you doing?" the earl asked.

Derringer glanced down at his pocket. "What, this? I need things to fence."

"Fence your own bloody possessions, you lackwit."

"I can't. No one knows I'm in England except you." He frowned. "And your new family."

"They will keep mum." He studied Derringer closely, noticing the signs of strain around the dark eyes. "Why must it be kept secret?" he asked, not really expecting an answer.

He didn't get one. Instead, the duke said, "I believe you have a visitor."

It was no surprise when Jamieson suddenly entered, announcing the Reverend Dr. Buckley. Derringer always did have uncanny hearing.

"Jamieson, inform her ladyship of the good reverend's arrival."

Lord Holt greeted his guest, indulging in some inane chatter. Turning about, Gideon realized his friend had slipped out.

He shrugged. It was just as well. Derringer would most likely have done something unpardonable, such as kiss Malvina.

Which only served to remind him that in a few hours, that would be his privilege. The mere thought made him turn to the door, anticipating his imminent marriage far more than he should.

With an abruptness unusual in the earl, he excused himself to his guest and left the room. He needed to change into something more appropriate and he needed to see Malvina, an urging inside him that he didn't understand.

What he didn't understand made him nervous. When he was nervous, he was jumpy, anxious, the complete opposite of the man he presented to Society.

He realized with a sinking feeling in his stomach that he was more like Derringer than he'd ever thought possible.

Jamieson met him—almost running over him, in fact —in the corridor, handing him a sealed note.

"This was left for you, my lord."

Gideon knew before he opened it that it was from Derringer.

He scanned the few words, bit off the curse hovering on his tongue, and crumpled the vellum in his hand.

"Where is Lady Malvina?"

"Her ladyship's maid said her ladyship would be down presently, my lord."

Gideon nodded. She was still in her chamber. Good. "That will be all, Jamieson."

As soon as the butler was out of sight, Lord Holt made his way to Malvina's room.

He didn't knock. The maid squeaked when he threw open the door.

"Out."

He was grimly aware that he'd managed to frighten the maid out of her wits. She fled as if pursued by Satan himself, slamming the door as she went.

He really must take care or he would be considered as balmy as Derringer.

Malvina stood at her dressing table, strands of dark red hair draped artistically over one shoulder. He had a lovely view of her naked back where she stood, half turned away. Maddy must have been fastening the long row of buttons down her mistress's back; the better part of them were still undone.

If he hadn't known better, Gideon would have searched her chambers for a male companion, such was her appearance. Her lack of corset was quite a scandalous decision on her part.

She looked alarmed, but not frightened. "What is it?" she asked, turning toward him, her bodice drooping precariously. Her hand automatically went up to hold it in place. "Is it Wolf?"

"In a manner of speaking, yes." Gideon forced his eyes away from the tempting picture she made. But staring in the direction of her bed was a mistake. "He is not hurt, however." *Yet*, he added to himself.

Malvina blushed. "Oh, dear. What has he done now?"

The sound Gideon made resembled something between a snort and a growl. Malvina's brow creased. She twisted one arm behind her back, trying to hold her gown closed, cursing inwardly at the slipperiness of the pale silk.

Turning redder still, she ventured, "My lord, could you help me?"

Gideon's eyes locked on her and he wondered briefly if he was being punished for some past wrong. He moved up behind her, flexing his hands, trying to quell the urge to remove the gown instead of doing it up.

He reached toward her, his fingers brushing lightly over her satin skin, lingering near the small of her back. He fastened one button, stepping even closer, fascinated by the shiver that rippled across her flesh.

He leaned closer, his breath on her neck. "Are you cold?"

Malvina managed an infinitesimal shake of her head. She was anything but cold. Her body felt over warm, almost feverish. She was acutely aware of him behind her, knew that all she had to do was turn ever so slightly and raise her lips to his, let her gown slip to the floor.

Squeezing her eyes shut, she fought for control. In a matter of minutes, they would be married and she could let her desires take control. She would not succumb to a man she did not call husband.

A tiny exhalation slipped out when his lips pressed intimately against her neck. Her mind told her to distract him, turn his attention away from seduction.

"Gideon." Her voice was soft, breathy, nearly trembling as his lips traced a path over her jaw and to her ear.

"Yes?"

She said the first thing that came to mind. "I am sorry about Black."

Mentioning his horse did have the desired effect. He managed to fasten the buttons in short order, only lingering over her skin for a brief second.

"You did nothing," was his reply.

Stepping back, Gideon forced his thoughts back to the newest threat to his family.

"Derringer has informed me of something I wish you had told me."

Malvina turned fully, her face showing a certain amount of trepidation with lingering traces of passion.

"Told you what?"

"That Wolf may have killed his father."

19

They were married in short order. Jamieson and his wife stood witness, the former straight and proud in his dark livery, the latter plump and motherly, her face beaming with happiness.

Malvina forced Gideon's revelation from her mind, not daring to believe there was any truth in the claim. She focused on the man at her side, tried to determine how she could feel safe and threatened at the same time.

After his accusation had drained her body of color and nearly the remainder of her senses, she had been tempted to call off the wedding, such as it was.

Her immediate defense of her only child had been concise and biting; Gideon had accepted it with what she could only call relief. But there had been something in his manner that suggested he did not necessarily believe her. His relief stemmed from some other fear. And Malvina withheld the information that Wolf was as much Brackney's victim as she was, that Wolf was the one who discovered his father, dead, all those years ago.

Shaking away the terror of that night, Malvina focused wholly on the present. She spoke the same words she'd spoken so many years before, when she was still a girl, little more than a child, words that had held meaning for her even then.

Despite her immaturity, she had been raised to believe vows were meant to be kept. Vows before God held more meaning than those before men. She had always felt a certain amount of failure when she'd never managed to love her first husband. And even though he had treated her abominably, part of her still felt guilty.

Lord Holt's voice when he spoke was easy, lacking any hesitation. She realized with a start that he felt no qualms at all about marrying her. Which meant one of two things: He either believed her completely innocent of her husband's activities, or he had no reservations about making vows he had no intention of keeping.

What a lowering thought that was!

She felt herself being turned, felt her new husband's lips press briefly to her fingers, and tried to ignore the disloyal thought that she may have made a colossal mistake.

Immediately following, the reverend was invited to dine and they all shared a rather stilted meal.

Wolf darted angry little glances at his mother and new stepfather, taking bites of food between glares. He was clearly displeased that the marriage had come to fruition and frustrated that he could do nothing about it.

Malvina grimaced at the eels in cream sauce, a dish she personally loathed. She concentrated on eating bite after bite, focusing all her attention on keeping it down. It gave her some relief from the new troubles plaguing her mind.

It was her wedding night. While she had no qualms about her desire for her husband, she did not like the way he looked at her son as though he was already found guilty of some crime. Her logical mind—not to mention her experience with Gideon to date—told her that even if he suspected, he would not harm the boy. Therefore, to feel guilty for desiring his lovemaking was illogical.

Malvina drained her wineglass and accepted another helping of eels, caring little what the others thought of her sudden appetite.

Gideon ate nothing. His wine glass was refilled several times, however, each new one disappearing quicker than the last. He alternately eyed his wife and stepson, wondering dismally why he felt so strongly that she was innocent and that her son was guilty.

It would have been preferable had he suspected her. Malvina Brackney—Holt, he reminded himself with an odd twinge—was incredibly protective of her son. Far more so than most mothers whose sons neared manhood. It hinted at some sort of trauma in the boy's past, something his mother didn't believe he could endure on his own.

He leaned back slightly, sliding down a little in his chair, lazy and indolent, allowing his mind to dwell on the puzzle.

His focus began with young Sir Beowulf Brackney, baronet.

The young man had a violent streak, a ready temper that was likely to explode over the smallest wrongs, real or imagined. He seemed to have little control over his emotions. It was dangerous in one so large and yet so young.

Derringer's note had been blunt. Gideon knew the duke's sources were uncannily accurate and he hated that in implying the boy had murdered his own father, Derringer had practically convicted him of the crime.

Although, if Gideon's superiors were correct, the late baronet was better off murdered by his son than standing trial for treason.

Allowing his eyelids to droop, he turned to study his bride.

She steadily ate course after course, as if she hadn't eaten in quite some time. Gideon bit back a grin. He suspected his wife was more nervous than her expression let on.

He supposed he'd be nervous, too, if his only experience in the bedchamber had been with a selfish partner with whom he could not connect on an emotional level.

Firmly putting that thought in the back of his mind, he drained his wineglass again and held it out to be refilled. He nodded absently at something the loquacious reverend had to say—indeed, he'd nearly forgotten the man was even there—and continued to stare quite rudely at the new Lady Holt.

She looked up, meeting his eyes. Hers widened a little. He could only imagine what she saw in his expression. She had the eerie ability to see through him, even while he was at his most opaque.

Looking from him to her son, her face flushed with every appearance of guilt and she looked away.

Gideon's face froze. She knew something. Or at least suspected. He would wager his life on it. Unfortunately, Lord Holt was very much afraid he might be doing just that.

"Well," the reverend said, complacently replete. "I must be going, my lord, my lady, sir." He smiled at each in turn, completely oblivious to the undercurrents in the room.

The room's occupants rose as one to see the man out. He refused to be seen to the door, assuring them all he knew the way. Seconds later, he was gone.

Gideon turned to Malvina. "Well, my dear. Perhaps you are ready to retire?"

She seemed surprised by the request but nodded her head, trying to prevent the blush that threatened to stain her cheeks. Her embarrassment died a sudden death with her husband's next words.

"I need to speak with Wolf."

Her head snapped up. "No!"

Hiding his surprise at her vehemence, he mildly offered, "I have no intention of harming him, my love."

"Yes, you do," she said defiantly. "I know why you wish to speak to him and I won't allow it."

One blond brow arched and he opened his mouth to reply. The subject of their argument, however, decided he didn't care to be spoken of as though he wasn't there.

"I am not afraid to speak with him, Mother, if you would dare to loosen the apron strings long enough. Bloody hell, you'd think I was still in shortcoats!"

"Language!"

Wolf scowled at them both. "My language is probably not what your *husband* wants to discuss," he remarked with obvious aversion.

Malvina's mouth opened and closed. "Very well," she finally said. Fixing her new husband with a minatory glare, she told her son, "If he hurts you, we will leave."

The wolfish smirk that Gideon was treated to for this piece of wifely disloyalty made the earl bite back a curse. How the devil was he to get the son to trust him if the mother refused?

"I will walk you to your chamber," he told Malvina firmly.

She felt a sinking in her midsection. The statement had slipped off her tongue without thought. Reflecting on the implications of her words—and viewing the smug look on her son's face—she realized the enormity of the mistake she had made.

Giving Wolf as stern a look as she was capable, she meekly followed her new husband from the room. She was pleased to note the shamefaced look that came over Wolf's countenance as she left. He was not entirely lost to sensitivity.

It was with only a little surprise that she found herself escorted almost roughly into a small salon that she realized with a start she'd never entered.

Upon entering, Gideon moved away, setting the candle he carried on a small table to the left of the door. Malvina used the opportunity to take a deep breath, preparing to explain her remark.

He turned and stared at her for a long moment, his expression completely unreadable. She opened her mouth to give some excuse, any excuse. The words that slipped out were not at all what either one of them expected.

"I love you."

The look of stupefied shock that crossed his dimly lit face must have been a direct reflection of her own.

He recovered quickly, however, saying, "If that is true —which at the moment, I give leave to doubt—you would trust me." He stepped closer. "You would trust me with your life and your son's." One more step and he was nearly touching her. His face was in heavy shadow, flecks of candle glow dancing in his brown eyes, the color a molten gold in the candle's flame.

He raised one hand to her face, his fingers curling over her cheek in an oddly possessive caress that made her skin tingle. She fought the sensations, knowing how important it was to stay in control.

He leaned down, bringing their faces level. His words feathered across her lips. "If you know me well enough to have fallen in love with me, you would know I could do nothing to willingly hurt a child, even one as hardheaded and vexing as your son."

"I do trust you. I am frightened."

She moved her head the required inch that was needed for their lips to meet. He hesitated only briefly, such a small amount of time that it mattered little. Then his free hand curved around her waist and she was pressed full-length against him. Heat touched her from chest to thigh, flames licking her skin and curling into her middle. She couldn't get close enough. Her fingers found his neckcloth, working the knot until she slid the starched linen from around his throat.

Both of his hands speared her hair, holding her head still as he ravished her mouth. Her hands slid over his bare throat, the accelerated beat of his heart fluttering against her fingertips. Moving down his chest, her arms wrapped around his waist.

A low growl rumbled in Gideon's throat. He pulled away, his breathing labored, a look of true regret on his face.

"As enticing as it is at this moment to forget you even have a son, and simply make love to you for the next year or two, I cannot."

Malvina stepped away, her sigh echoing his. Part of her had hoped to do just that, distract him away from his original purpose. She sighed again, nodding her head in defeat.

He pulled her chin up, forcing her to meet his shadowed eyes. "I will not hurt him, love. I want to help him."

His fingers stroked her jaw, his eyes searching hers for she knew not what. She was unsure how he could see anything in the light from only one candle anyway.

He kissed her lightly, and pointed to a door she hadn't noticed. "Your new room is through there. Maddy is waiting for you."

As he turned to leave, his voice floated back to her, but she couldn't be sure what he said. She thought she heard him say the one thing she longed to hear, but never believed she would.

It took everything in her not to chase after him and demand he repeat himself. Or explain. Or both.

Malvina came awake to the feel of warm lips pressed to hers and warm hands stroking heat through her body. The bed dipped as her new husband slid in beside her, drawing her into his arms and making love to her until the wee hours of the morning. He told her as many times as she could ever dream and showed her in ways she never thought possible that he loved her. Daylight peeked through the curtains when they fell, exhausted, into peaceful slumber.

The honeymoon that had never really started was officially over less than three hours later. They were awakened by a distraught maid and informed that Wolf was missing.

# 20

So married life wasn't progressing quite as happily as Gideon could have hoped. He grimaced slightly, urging his wife's maid to rid the chamber of the fouled bed linens. His bride groaned, acutely embarrassed, no doubt, to have cast up her accounts all over the bed—and him.

The maid bobbed a curtsy, leaving the chamber with her unwanted burden.

Lord Holt glanced down at himself and quickly away, feeling a little sick. He swiped ineffectually at his chest with a damp cloth. It was not the most prodigious beginning to a new day.

Approaching the bed, he said consolingly, "It is of no account, my love. Under the circumstances, the like is to be expected."

She twisted her beautiful face into a mask of disgust. "If that were the case, you and the servants would have stood ready with a chamberpot."

Gideon smiled slightly. "I suggest we bathe and dress quickly. Unless I miss my guess, Hart will be arriving this morning. He'll have heard by now, since the servants know."

Malvina gasped and moved to throw back the blankets, heedless of her nakedness. She dived back under when the door opened, her maid returning to inform her of the bath awaiting her in her own chamber.

A short chuckle escaped her husband as she exited to refresh herself.

It was with a certain amount of surprise and dread that the newlyweds realized the Duke of Derringer was not coming. If he had already left the city, they may never know what was happening.

By afternoon, Gideon realized he had to take care of certain other matters, promising to look into the situation with Malvina's son while he was out. He strongly suspected the boy was just spreading his wings, venturing into the many vices London life had to offer.

While Gideon could not condone such a thing, he also knew the futility of trying to hold down a sixteen-year-old boy who possessed the power of a mastiff when threatened.

Searching for dissipation or not, there were certain things that could not wait.

He had his carriage brought round and instructed the coachman to take him to the Home Office. Once there, he asked the assistant to see the Home Secretary and waited.

Twenty minutes later, he was ushered into the Home Secretary's presence. He greeted Lord Sidmouth briefly before coming to the material point.

"Brackney's widow is innocent and I can find no evidence of Brackney's guilt," he said, taking the seat offered by his superior. He refrained from confiding the boy's disappearance, a circumstance Gideon saw as irrelevant but Lord Sidmouth might find suspicious.

"What of the son?"

"Sir Beowulf? He is a hotheaded child, nothing more. At this date, I suspect he has little more than a guilty conscience for killing my horse." *Although, there are certain other things alluded to by Derringer that bear looking into,* he thought.

The older man's brows rose at this but Gideon did not feel compelled to explain his cryptic remark. Instead, he continued.

"I was intrigued to note, however, that her ladyship was being blackmailed. Considering she did not know of her husband's activities but knew what he was capable of, it was only natural that she believe the incentive was legitimate."

"What has that to do with your mission?"

Gideon smiled in his oddly lazy way. "Maybe nothing. Maybe everything. Who's to say?"

"Who is blackmailing her?"

Frowning, the earl's reply was less than satisfactory. "I am working on that, my lord. He may or may not be the man we have been looking for. He is not in control, however."

"There is someone above him? Brackney's contact, no doubt."

"If Brackney was involved, which I still doubt."

The Home Secretary eyed him shrewdly. "Are you able to complete your mission, Holt?"

A spurt of annoyance lit in Gideon's breast at the mild slur on his honor. "Of course, my lord. There is nothing preventing me from obtaining a satisfactory answer to your enigma."

"Anything else?"

"No, sir."

Lord Sidmouth grunted and waved his subordinate from the room.

As Gideon stood, he said, "Wish me happy, my lord. I am to but recently married."

The other man smiled slightly, distractedly. "Who is she?"

"The former Lady Richard Brackney."

A moment of stunned silence passed. "Dammit, Holt! Have you lost your wits? I cannot have my best man murdered in his bed by a treasonous female."

Gideon's sleepy expression slipped into place. "She is innocent, my lord," was all he said in his own defense.

Lord Sidmouth's lips tightened in annoyance. "What if it is proven that Brackney betrayed his country?"

"I am well aware of the law, my lord. But if I am the likely one to prove her late husband a traitor, the least I can do is help her in any way I can."

"But marriage? You could have set her up as your mistress, man. That's all she'd be good for after the gossipmongers sink their teeth into her."

Gideon chose not to respond to his superior's provoking suggestion. "Is there anything else, sir?"

"No, off with you. Catch your man and dam up this wellspring. I have other things to attend to."

After Gideon left, Malvina paced.

She paced the drawing room floor endlessly, always moving to look to the street, eager for news.

She had sent servants out to inquire after her son and they soon returned, one by one, to shake their heads sadly at their new mistress and promise to try harder.

She was at her wit's end. Something inside her would not let her rest. A sick gnawing in her stomach told her clearly that she did not believe her son had simply gone out on a lark, as her new husband had tried to reassure her.

What kind of reassurance was that, anyway, to a mother who did nothing but worry?

As she paced by the door, she was nearly knocked down as Jamieson entered to hand her a note. Praying it was from Gideon, informing her of her son's safety, she was unprepared for the shock that traveled the length of her body.

The words seemed to jump out at her. Her body seemed to lose solidarity. She sank down, thankfully she was close enough to a chair that Jamieson could slide it beneath her.

"It can't be," she whispered, her words barely audible.

"My lady?"

Her face lifted to the butler's, too shocked for tears. "He's dead, Jamieson."

Austere features crumpling into something more human and less servile, the butler so far forgot himself to ask, "Who?"

"Wolf, my son, my child—"

Darting panicked glances around a room that was empty of humanity except for Lady Holt and himself, Jamieson saw no alternative but to assist her in any way he could. He moved to the bellpull and then returned to his mistress's side, handing her a glass of sherry, hoping to restore some color to her pale cheeks.

Malvina accepted it gratefully, downing it in a single swallow, barely conscious of her surroundings. She was then dimly aware of servants entering, maids clucking over her, bustling her from the room.

She went willingly enough. Indeed, she did not know what else she could do. Except...

"Jamieson," she said, pausing in the doorway, "who delivered this?"

"A gentleman, madam."

"A gentleman?"

"Yes, madam. The gentleman declined to enter, implying certain obligations elsewhere."

"How very curious," she murmured, her face not matching her words.

"My lord has been sent for, my lady," Jamieson inserted, hoping to erase some of the blank expression from her face.

"Very good, Jamieson," Malvina said dutifully, her mind a whirligig of ideas. She left the room, not revealing the insane idea that had crowded, foremost, in her mind.

Upon entering her room, she dismissed her maid. Maddy left reluctantly, her pleasant face revealing her concern for her mistress.

Malvina swiftly fetched outer clothing from her wardrobe, sufficient for hiding most of her appearance. She had some errands to run, one of which involved scouring certain parts of London where no lady had any business, nor did gentlemen for that matter.

She had to find him. If anyone knew the truth, it was him.

21

When Gideon received the summons to return home, he was shocked. Whatever he was expecting, it was not the insanity that greeted him upon his arrival.

The house was in an uproar. Servants ran hither and thither, seemingly without purpose, shouting to each other as if Bedlam had erupted within the confines of Berkeley Square.

"What in bloody hell!" he exclaimed when a footman nearly knocked him back into the street.

He quickly recovered, the footman alternately stammering out apologies and shouting for Mr. Jamieson.

The butler hurried out, his face drawn with worry. "Oh, my lord, thank God!"

"What has happened, Jamieson?" the earl inquired with deceptive mildness.

"Her ladyship received a note, my lord. She went to her chamber, we thought to lie down but she sent Maddy away. When Maddy went to check on her, she was gone!"

Gideon felt his heart stop. The good butler's words tumbled out, one over the other, almost too fast for his master to comprehend. It was not much for Gideon to grasp the key point.

"Where is the note?"

It was handed to him immediately, Jamieson hovering, awaiting orders.

They were not long in coming. As Gideon strode through the heavy front door into the darkening street beyond, he issued orders with all the bearing of a general.

"Send a message round to Derringer's residence. Determine if anyone has seen him. We need the duke's expertise."

The butler opened his mouth to call a footman but closed it abruptly, a look of utter shock crossing his features.

A carriage was stopped before the earl's residence, a pair of demonic black horses stamping and pawing the ground in their unhappiness with their lot in life. A man in black leapt down, his saturnine features as bland as ever.

"That won't be necessary, Witless."

Gideon breathed a sigh of relief, for once giving little heed to the despised appellation that Derringer always employed.

"Hart, where is she?"

The duke turned, offering his hand to someone who still sat in the carriage behind him. "She is safe, Holt," he said, almost kindly.

Lady Malvina stepped down, her face tear-stained and blotchy. Gideon stepped forward, lifting her into his arms.

Looking over her head at the duke, he asked, "It is true, then?"

Derringer nodded. "It is."

They moved to enter the house, the duke following.

"Deverell?"

Derringer's snort spoke volumes. "I do hope you told Sidmouth of his crimes?"

"I did not, in so many words."

Reaching out, Derringer stopped his friend just outside the drawing room door. "You did not?"

"No. Why?"

"Why didn't you?" the duke countered. "Did you not have the proof of his treachery? What stopped you?"

"Fear for Malvina and Wolf."

Derringer gave him a long, probing look before firmly ushering them into the drawing room, quite as if he was the master, not Lord Holt.

Malvina was deposited on the settee, her husband gently brushing the hair back from her brow, murmuring some low words for her ears alone. He turned to ring for Maddy and was only mildly surprised to see her immediately behind him.

"Please tend to your mistress," he said. "His grace and I will be in the study."

A few minutes later, the gentlemen were deep in discussion.

Gideon held his head in his hands, deeply distressed and blaming himself. "I thought the boy was just out sowing his wild oats. I never believed Deverell would do something like this."

"We don't even know yet what he's done," Derringer pointed out unhelpfully.

Moving to a table in the corner, he filled two tumblers with brandy and took one back to his friend.

"Do you want me to find Deverell?"

Gideon looked at Derringer. "Of course I do. I want him dead for what he's done."

"Treason?"

Gideon swore fluently. "It is not my right, is it?"

The duke shrugged. He had little use for the monarchy, such as it was, and made no secret of that fact. "You did not hand over your proof yet. One could say that you do not have it at this moment and did away with a murderer before you discovered the proof you needed."

"It won't answer," Gideon said reluctantly. He rose to his feet and proceeded to refill his glass. Tossing back the contents, he added, "I have already been instructed to investigate him. If he suddenly dies at my hand, it would cause too many questions."

"Fatal mishap?"

The earl shook his head. "Too coincidental, Hart."

The duke set aside his glass. "It is settled then."

"What is?"

Derringer's features creased into a smile that his friends knew meant trouble. "What is *what*, my dear sir?"

The feeling that assailed Gideon was relief mixed with frustration. As much as everything in him screamed out for Deverell to feel justice at his own hand, he knew it was much better for everyone if Lord Heartless took care of everything.

A visit to the Home Office the following day did little to solve Gideon's family troubles. There had been no sign of Lord Delwyn Deverell in all the time the Holts had been resident in London. It was decidedly odd, to say the least.

And yet, he had been there. It was unlikely that he could elude everyone, but it seemed to be exactly what he had managed.

He had had to endure a blistering scold from Lord Sidmouth, ultimately resulting in Lord Holt's resigning his position with the Home Office. The two gentlemen had agreed it was probably for the best, with the earl newly married.

The news he'd received just before leaving had almost made the visit worthwhile. But not quite.

Gideon returned home, disheartened. For the first time since he'd married, he did not want to see Malvina. He did not want to see her face again, see that expression that cut so deep it was indescribable.

And it was all his fault. If he had taken Deverell's evil tendencies more seriously, he could have prevented this tragedy.

It was inconceivable that Deverell could be so lost to humanity. He had been a quiet boy, never drawing attention to himself, enduring Derringer's overly cruel teasing with a calm that was extraordinary in one so young.

Gideon frowned, entering his study. Deverell had been an odd child. He had never seemed to care about anything, was always indifferent. He had watched but rarely participated; been a follower but rarely a doer.

Why had he associated with Derringer's crowd in the first place?

Shaking his head at the futility of trying to determine why a killer and traitor would do the things he did, Gideon sat down at his desk. Sitting on top, in plain view, was a folded sheet of vellum.

The handwriting was a familiar memory from his school days.

He reached out to take it, his hand almost moving of its own accord. His mind screamed for him to stop, to avoid the news he was sure was contained within.

He swore. It was not what he had expected, neither was it good.

Derringer would arrive within hours.

Gideon met him at the door.

"Did you find him?"

"I did. He will not be killing anymore young men." A hint of satisfaction brightened Derringer's black eyes.

"What of Wolf?"

It was not a pleasant thing that Gideon saw reflected in the duke's face. It was an expression of hopeless despair. It was a failure that Derringer couldn't right, one that involved the death of a child, a child that he had secretly admired even while he pitied him.

"I do not know what to say, Holt. I have too many reports of a large young man of Wolf's description meeting his untimely demise at the hands of robbers in the rookeries."

Gideon swallowed hard. "What of his body?"

"Gone," the duke replied succinctly. "Two men whose word I trust saw him tossed into the Thames."

"What?"

The gentlemen turned to see Lady Holt, her face a mask of horror and dashed hope. Derringer's response was to curse roundly and storm out, brushing roughly by her as he fled the room.

Gideon's reaction was a little less dramatic but no less heartfelt.

He crossed the room to stand before her, framing her stricken face with his hands. Leaning forward until their heads touched, he whispered, "I am so sorry, my love."

22

It was some months before Malvina was able to accept her son's death. Gideon watched her closely, terrified for her and unsure how to help her. He didn't know the pain of losing a child though he mourned the loss of hers. Wolf had been irritating, hotheaded, and generally uncontrollable, but he'd loved his mother and tried to protect her as best he could. Gideon could hardly fault him for that.

London palled so they packed up and returned to Moorview Park. Malvina and the Dowager avoided each other, which seemed to work for all involved.

It was a week after their arrival that Gideon realized just how clever a decision it was. In his desire to remove her from the prying eyes and whispering tongues of Society, he'd actually struck upon the perfect solution for her grief.

Samantha.

They held each other up. The girl had formed an attachment to Wolf that no one had anticipated. She grieved but her grief allowed her to accept the outcome and comfort the new countess, her sister-in-law.

Gideon stood in the library, a brandy in one hand. He occasionally lifted the glass to his lips, even occasionally tasted the fine amber liquid that touched his tongue. But for the most part, his mind refused to settle, and so preoccupied was he that not only didn't he taste his drink, he also didn't hear the door open behind him.

"Giddy?"

He turned at the soft tone, the usual heartache snaking through him. "Sammy." Soft blue wool draped her body, smudges of dirt on the bodice and skirt. She'd no doubt been in the stables, and not realized she carried some of the dirt in with her.

It was time she married, he mused. His friend Trent would make her a good husband, but Gideon wasn't sure if either one of them still approved the match. Samantha was but a child when the betrothal was arranged. But she would turn eighteen later in the year and should be thinking about a family of her own rather than tending to his.

She grimaced at the pet name but Gideon couldn't be sorry. He adored his sister and would never forgive himself for his part in her disfigurement. She would always be 'Sammy' to him, reminding him of a time when she was perfect.

"I hate that name, Giddy," she remarked, moving forward to slide a finger over the brandy decanter. If he didn't know better, he'd think she wanted a drink.

He shrugged and stepped to her side, setting his empty glass on the table and pulling the stopper from the decanter. "As I hate that name?" He sloshed three fingers into his glass, then, after a slight hesitation, he sloshed little more than a mouthful into another glass and handed it to his sister.

She stared at it, then glanced at him. A tear slipped down her cheek as she accepted the offering. She tossed it back as she'd seen her brother do, coughing at the burn in her throat.

Gideon thumped her on the back, smiling. "Harsh, no?"

Her laugh bubbled up between gasps and coughs. "Horrid stuff, Giddy! How can you stand it?"

He shrugged one shoulder, a tinge of darkness settling over his features. "It grows on one." Thus saying, he downed his drink and set the glass on the table.

A shudder racked her small frame. "I do not think so." She carefully set her glass down, then grasped the table edge as the spirits went straight to her head. "Oh my," she whispered.

Gideon helped her to a chair. "Have you eaten anything today?" At Samantha's brief head shake, he mused, "Perhaps that mouthful was a bit too much for you, love." She nodded, then shook her head as if she could shake away the dizziness. He sat beside her and clasped her hand, for once not allowing himself to look away from her scarred features, the scars he caused.

"Giddy, I have his horse."

He almost didn't catch her low whisper. Then, with a sinking in his middle, he asked, "Whose horse?"

Though he'd been home for nearly a month, he'd neglected his stables. Even when he spent time there, he barely noticed new additions, as it was Samantha's domain. He had his animals and she had hers. Besides that, horses now reminded him of Wolf and his own ineffectually brief time as a stepfather. He fought the desire to curse a blue streak.

"Wolf's Grendel."

Of course his sister would still get the boy a horse. She'd probably had the beast for months, just waiting for Wolf's return. Tears tightened Gideon's throat even as he barked a laugh. "Grendel? You named Beowulf's horse Grendel?"

Samantha smiled but her tears seeped from the corners of her eyes. "He's an ugly, spotted beast that Hollings found," she explained, referring to their stable master. "He was looking at a hunter I'd heard was up for auction and when he saw Grendel he thought of Wolf and recalled your orders to get him a horse. I thought—I thought Wolf would like him. I changed his name to the one name I thought suited horse and master. I thought—" Her hands tightened on her brother's, her lip trembling. "Oh, Giddy, I was so vexed with him. I thought he was a horrid boy and deserved to be punished. But I never—"

Gideon released her hands to draw her into his arms, tucking her head beneath his chin. "He would have loved Grendel, Sammy." Gideon sighed. "He admired you. I think he was a little in love with you."

That particular revelation sent her into choking sobs. Gideon held her, stroking her hair, wondering where his wife was and if Samantha did this while in her company. He suspected the girl held it all in, out of consideration for Malvina, saving her tears for the privacy of her own chamber. Had no one held her? He'd not thought about it, never considered Samantha might not have anyone to hold her up the way she tended to hold up everyone else. He knew Malvina would have, had she been less wrapped in her own grief.

As if summoned, Malvina entered, a wide smile lighting her pale features. It was the first smile he'd seen on her face since Wolf's disappearance. And though far less than six months had passed, she'd set aside her mourning attire, choosing a white muslin gown edged with Pomona green silk. Gracing her throat was the pearl pendant he'd bestowed upon her just after he met her, matching gems—a gift he'd had commissioned just after their marriage—sparkling at her ears.

Samantha composed herself, easing out of her brother's arms and turning to face Malvina. Gideon rose to his feet, his sister following suit. Her face brightened considerably. "You are looking well."

Malvina's eyes remained fixed on her husband, though she did greet the young woman at his side. Then, "Gideon, I must speak with you."

Samantha excused herself. As she passed by Malvina, she impulsively hugged her. "I am pleased you are feeling better." She left, closing the door behind her.

Gideon eyed his wife, not entirely sure what to expect. Over the course of several weeks he'd been treated in turns to rage, silence, tears, and indifference. Her rage had even spilled over onto Derringer, driving that man into hiding.

This radiant creature before him was one he'd never seen in the short time he'd known her.

She placed her hands over her belly, her lips parting as she gazed at him. "It's happened, my love. There will be a child—Ooo!"

He'd crossed the room and scooped her up before she'd finished speaking. Kissing her soundly, he returned her to her feet, unable to hold back his joyous grin.

"When?"

"September." Joy, contentment, and peace settled over her features, tinged with a weary sadness. "I only wish Wolf was here to share this. I know he'd love to have a brother or sister."

Gideon wasn't sure if it was the baby that caused Malvina's acceptance of Wolf's death or if she'd just lost hope. She'd maintained from the start that he was alive, even after Derringer's claim to the contrary.

As if reading his mind, she said, "I think he's alive, Gideon. I will never accept his...death."

Gideon nodded. "I understand, my love. I'm not sure I believe he's gone either." It was a lie. Gideon knew, deep down, that Wolf was gone. But if it helped Malvina to believe otherwise, he'd accept that.

"I have news," he revealed, "something I should have told you months ago." He took her hand and led her to the settee he'd just occupied with his sister. "Seems Brackney wasn't a traitor. His name is cleared, as is that of Wolf."

"Not a traitor?" Malvina repeated, brow furrowed. "But what of the journal Deverell said he possessed?"

"Deverell lied," Gideon stated, stifling the fury he felt at the mere thought of that bounder. The man was dead and gone, but Gideon still hated the mere memory of him. "There was never a journal because Brackney knew better than to keep such a thing."

Malvina nodded. "So those hold-ups"—her voice trembled on the words—"were nothing more than a means to fund Deverell's escape?" She knew that. It was still horrifying to think of *That Man* using her simply to help his own escape from a well-deserved fate.

"So it would seem."

"And what of my part, Gideon? Shall I pay for my crimes?"

"Sidmouth has no interest beyond those who employed Deverell. Even Deverell is but a means of finding the ringleaders. I've convinced him that you and Wolf were but unfortunate pawns. And I've made some recompense to the family of the boy who died."

Malvina swallowed tears. "I would like to apologize to the family for my part in their son's death."

Gideon squeezed her hand. "I have done so. They were most understanding."

Malvina shrugged away from him, rising to her feet. "How can that be so?" In her agitation, she paced to the small table where the brandy decanter sat. Wrapping her fingers around the container's neck, she lifted it, pulling the stopper out. "How can any parent forgive such a crime against their child?" She splashed the smallest amount into one of the provided glasses, set the decanter aside, and lifted the glass, staring into the pale amber liquid coating the bottom. "How can they forgive me for the part I played in the loss of their child?"

"They do not know," Gideon whispered, his voice close to her ear. She'd not realized he'd moved from his place across the room. "I told them of the hold-up, of their son's willingness to assist you despite the danger to himself." He gently removed the glass from her fingers. "They are happy knowing their son—a young man who'd previously shown no hint of unselfish behavior—was willing to risk his life to assist a lady in danger. He died a hero. It is all they need to know."

Malvina closed her eyes, taking in deep breaths with lungs that almost refused to allow it. Eyes flying wide, she retrieved the glass from her husband and downed the tiny bit of brandy she'd poured. Heat spiraled into her stomach, sending a warm fuzziness into her brain. It wasn't her first taste of brandy and it wouldn't be her last but it was all she needed at the moment. A calming lassitude invaded her limbs and she could breathe again. The glass barely rattled as she set it on the table.

There was a reason for everything, she reminded herself. Smiling, Malvina turned to her husband and cupped his cheek, forcing his eyes to meet hers. "As much as I hate the agony Deverell has caused, I cannot regret the past. I cannot regret meeting you."

"Have you considered I am the reason you lost your son?"

Her smile faltered, just a bit. His face shuttered, hiding his feelings from her though she knew his pain, his guilt, ran as deep as hers. "We cannot know if things would have been different for Wolf had we never met you," she soothed, her fingers tracing a path over the worry lines framing his mouth. "It does not do to blame yourself, love."

His lips brushed over her fingertips. "No amount of logic can overcome guilt. I wish I could have saved him."

The pain in his words sent agony through Malvina's chest, stealing her breath. This man loved her despite her sins, despite the sins of her son or husband. He loved her, loved her son, and his joy at the impending child told her he already loved it. She would take his pain from him, if she could, and he'd proven he'd take hers.

"You did save him. He admired you. You were what he needed in his life, a father who cared more for him than he cared for himself." She raised up on her toes in an attempt to better meet his gaze, willing him to accept her assurances. "Never feel otherwise."

It was a long moment that the two stared at each other. Gideon's smile went straight to her heart. "I love you, Lady Holt." He kissed her softly, the chaste salute sending warmth through her.

Malvina smiled against his lips and pulled away just enough to assure him, "I love you, Lord Holt."

Several minutes later, Malvina sighed, lifting her head to look at her husband. "With Deverell gone, one can't help but wonder what happened to all that money he stole."

"It was never found. I couldn't begin to guess where he might have been hiding it. Now, no more talk of Deverell."

# EPILOGUE

*Several years later...*

The Indian sun blazed down on Lord Delwyn Deverell's back. Hooking his cane over his arm, he swept his hat from his head and wiped the perspiration from his brow, eyes squinting into the sky. How he hated this Godforsaken country with its insects and heat! Surely it was hell itself, risen to the surface.

It mattered naught. He'd endured India's heat in the years since Holt nearly caught him with his hand in the government's cookie jar, but that was over now.

His gaze swept the port, landing on the ship that would take him back to England. He leaned heavily on his cane, dark thoughts swirling. His leg didn't heal properly after his last run-in with the Duke of Derringer. That madman would pay for what he did.

Rage swept through Deverell's veins. He'd not even known Derringer was in London until the man attacked him in the rookeries. Several unconscious hours later, he'd awakened to a vagrant going through his pockets.

Dispatching that blighter to his maker had taken nothing more than a flick of the wrist on Deverell's part. It was when he struggled to stand that he realized that black devil had done more than just beat him. He'd broken his leg. A painful limp would forever remind him of his hatred for the Duke of Derringer.

A soft breeze ruffled his hair. Replacing his hat, he boarded the boat. England—no, *vengeance* beckoned.

# ABOUT THE AUTHOR

Jaimey Grant, a pseudonym for Laura Miller, was born in Michigan in 1979. After a fun-filled childhood interlaced with moments of emotional trauma and an insatiable curiosity about the reasons people act the way they do, she became a writer.

Primarily a Regency romance author, Jaimey has also dabbled in fantasy of a non-romance variety. A comprehensive list of works and where to find them can be found on her website, www.jaimeygrant.com. There are more Regencies and fantasies in the works.

She currently lives in Michigan with her husband and two children.

To learn more about Jaimey and her work, visit any of the sites below.

Website: http://www.jaimeygrant.com
Facebook: http://www.facebook.com/jaimeygrantauthor
Email: jaimeygrant@yahoo.com

CPSIA information can be obtained
at www.ICGtesting.com
Printed in the USA
LVHW080452050123
736521LV00013B/465

9 781617 521744